FALLING
FOR
THE VILLAIN

FALLING

FOR THE VILLAIN

WALL STREET JOURNAL & USA TODAY BESTSELLING AUTHOR

M. ROBINSON

#1 *New York Times* Bestselling Author

RACHEL VAN DYKEN

Falling For The Villain
by M. Robinson & Rachel Van Dyken

FALLING FOR THE VILLAIN
Copyright © 2021 M. ROBINSON & RACHEL VAN DYKEN
ISBN: 978-1-946061-88-1
Cover Design & Editing by Silla Webb, Masque of the Red Pen
Formatting & Editing by Jill Sava, Love Affair With Fiction

AUTHOR NOTE

We are so pumped to bring you guys Falling For The Villain! Full disclosure, things took an insane turn the minute we started writing it and quite honestly couldn't stop even though it was nothing like we had planned (Isn't that the best sort of story though?)

*This story is not for the faint of heart and may be uncomfortable for some readers. But, then again, stepping outside of your comfort zone may be exactly the thing you need…

Care to play with us, readers?

♥ XOXO, M. Robinson & RVD

DEDICATION

For anyone who's ever fallen for a villain

PROLOGUE

Present Day

"Play for me, Juliet."

Those were the first four words he ever said to me. I used to loathe those words.

Each letter.

Each syllable.

Word for word.

Until one day, I started counting down the hours until I played for him again. There once was a time when I despised everything about him. From his dark black, seedy, daunting eyes that used to petrify me anytime he walked into my room. To the sound of his voice that was both calm and eerie, smooth and dominant, thrilling yet terrifying. His tone was sharp, clipped, and it didn't matter what he was spewing or demanding, whether it was hateful, punishing, or he was trying to please me; it was always precise and authoritative.

What I used to really hate the most about him, though, was how much he made me crave his touch, his torture. His presence was as consuming as the music I played for him.

It was all such a thin line.

Love and hate.

Happiness and sorrow.

Angel and demon.

Heaven and Hell.

I was raised in a world where I didn't know the difference. It all blended together, good versus evil.

"Play for me, Juliet."

My fingers trembled against the ivory keys of the Steinway Alma Tadema piano. Over a hundred thousand dollars were under the tips of my fingers. The devastatingly handsome man behind me was powerful.

Envied.

Feared by all.

Wearing an expensive tuxedo, he looked so pleased with himself as he stared out toward his guests for the evening.

I was playing front and center in the open room, where all eyes were on me wearing a clingy white silk gown. Flawlessly, I shifted my fingers from one key to the next, playing the piano like my life depended on it.

I guess in a way it did because he depended on it.

Music was always an escape for me. The piano was just another extension of my soul, my heart, my body. I needed the sanctuary that only the vibration of the keys provided. Getting lost in the symmetry was the only way I survived this long.

I was his doll.

His play toy.

He could do with me as he wanted, and trust me—he did often.

My hair was pinned back with a few soft waves framing my face. You see, my villain loved beautiful things, and I was just another object he prided himself on owning. So he did with me as he pleased. My role in his life was to grant him peace through the fucked up things he did to me.

I soaked up every last bit of attention he ever gave me.

I always did.

Every single caress.

Every single smile in my direction.

"Play," he said a second time, his hands coming down hard on my shoulders while I started playing "Reverie" by Debussy and Thibaudet.

People watched in rapture as my hands danced across the keys, and he stood proudly behind me as if I was just another piece of his collection, another prized possession.

All in a little game of catch with no release. I was now his property, a chess piece in a very dangerous game of cat and mouse.

With an end game that nobody could ever truly win.

He was incapable of love; he told me so the first day we met.

"I won't love you. Ever." His jaw clenched. "Make no mistake, though, your days as Juliet Sinacore are finished. But your days as my pet have only just begun."

"So beautiful, Juliet, so fucking beautiful," he rasped into my ear from behind me.

Beautiful but not broken.

I could take his brutality.

His sick, sinister games.

The fact that I belonged to him and always had.

I could take anything he ever gave me. Our relationship changed. It evolved. I was still very much his pet, and he was still my master in every sense of the word.

I loved him.

He loved me.

And a villain in love…

Was a very dangerous thing.

CHAPTER ONE

Juliet

The beginning

My eyes fluttered open, but all I could see was darkness.

Pitch. Black. Opaqueness.

I was in a blindfold. My hands were tied together behind my back, knocked unconscious on what felt like a solid chair. A slow throb started pulsing at my temples, reminding me I'd been hit on the head with something the minute I'd stepped on the beach. I was watching my nephew Naz for my brother and his wife while they were on their honeymoon.

Where was he? Did they take him too?

Panic quickly began to take hold, and the metallic taste of blood filled my mouth as I tried to lick against the tape that was pressed over my lips.

Caught off guard, I abruptly sat up, only to hear the keys of a piano go off.

Did they put me on a piano?

I couldn't scream.

I could barely move.

Who?

What?

Where?

I wondered briefly as pain slammed into my chest—*was this how I was going to die? Sitting at a piano?* My favorite thing to do in all the world.

My thoughts went back to the last conversation I had with my brother, Romeo. I'd been begging him to let me do my part in the family business for ages. He'd finally talked to my father, one of the main captains for the organized crime Sinacore family. All the 'men' decided I was too young, too inexperienced—too innocent.

I was naive.

A young woman.

A child in their eyes.

Though let's be honest—I'd practically breathed mafia life since the day I was born, but those weren't the reasons that really got to me.

"She's too pretty."

Like they were concerned some psychopath was going to carve out his name in my cheek, leaving me marked forever.

Tainted.

Broken.

Were they right?

I struggled again against the ropes.

Romeo must be so worried.

Behind the blindfold, I squeezed my eyes shut. I wouldn't cry. I couldn't give them the satisfaction. I'd just save up all those tears for later once I was rescued because I would be rescued; half of Seattle's most powerful men were more than likely already out looking for me.

Which begged the next plaguing question: *who would have the balls to take me?*

Tears streamed down my face.

More silence.

It was driving me crazy, the fucking quiet.

Maybe that was their point.

I'd either been taken by someone who saw an opportunity and went for it or by someone more devious. That thought alone sent shivers coursing down my spine and to the pit of my stomach.

Until I finally heard a deep voice order, "Play for me, Juliet."

How did he know I could play?

Hearing his voice did something to me, and I instantly started to fight against everything, especially the voice that was a few feet away from me. I must have been quite the pitiful sight, and I wasn't going to get loose unless he untied me; however, that wasn't going to stop me from trying.

"If you keep squirming like that, you'll only make yourself bleed, and I'm already not happy that my men split your temple. It would be in your best interest to not hurt yourself. I already killed two people today because they didn't follow my orders."

I fought the urge to hurl.

My stomach sank further when I realized how hopeless I truly was.

"I'm going to remove your blindfold and the tape over your mouth, but I need you to stay very still. I don't want to hurt you yet, but don't for one second think that I won't."

Yet?

The blindfold was pulled loose, and for a brief instant, I would have rather not known the man behind the crippling voice.

The room's dim lighting made it harder to see, and I wondered if he did that for me. Before I could continue with my mindless thoughts, the tape was crudely stripped from my mouth, and I screamed out in agony. All the illusions of this possibly being a dream became a nightmare within seconds.

"What do you say?" he rasped as I desperately tried to focus on the voice in front of me and not the stinging across my mouth.

How long have I been here that my eyes can't adjust that quickly?

"I didn't ask for questions, Juliet."

Did I say that out loud?

"Now, what do you say?"

I narrowed my eyes, trying to see the man hidden in the shadows. I couldn't see his face even though he was only standing a few feet away from me, but I knew even if I did get free, I wouldn't make it past him.

Running on pure adrenaline alone, I asked, "Who are you?"

The last word barely left my mouth when he tightly gripped my face and squeezed so hard I instantly whimpered out in pain.

"What. Do. You. Say?"

A muffled "Thank you" escaped from the dryness in my mouth.

"Good girl," he praised, instantly letting me go and allowing the blood to rush back to my cheeks. "I know you're scared," he added softly, his tone effortlessly altering to a calm voice. "All you have to do is be obedient, and no harm will ever come to you. If you don't listen to me, I'll be forced to punish you. The choice is yours. It's really quite simple, Juliet. Is that understood?"

My mind was working a million miles a minute.

"I really don't like waiting. I'm not a patient man, and you're testing my limits already."

"Yes..." I breathed out, my lips trembling. "I understand."

"You're such a good girl," he praised again with an annoyingly calm and patronizing tone that made me want to lunge at him.

The black dots around my eyes finally subsided, and I started to see things clearer, beginning with his cold, dark, seedy eyes staring back at me. It was the only emotion he wore.

Evil.

"I'm going to remove the binds on your hands. You won't fight me. If you do, you're going to learn very quickly that your actions have consequences, and I'm going to have to teach you your first lesson. Understood?"

My eyes filled with tears.

"Crying won't help you, and it won't save you either. I'm untouchable, Juliet. No one will find you, not even your mafia family and their ties."

Tears streamed down my face, one right after the other. When the back of his hand came toward my cheek, I instinctively jerked back, thinking he was going to hit me. He didn't. Ever so lightly, he wiped away my tears before slowly and casually licking them off his fingers.

"See, pet ... they belong to me now too."

My eyes widened.

This man had no remorse, not one shred of decency. There was no emotion in his eyes, no sympathy, and it was obvious he was getting off on the fact that I was scared.

"I know you may not believe me, but I can assure you that by the end of this, you'll not only be thanking me, but you'll also be in love with me. I'll even go as far as to say you'll die for me."

My heart beat heavily against my chest, pounding so hard and fast I thought I was going to pass out.

With the knuckles of his fingers, he swept the hair away from my face and shook his head in disappointment. I saw the blood on his fingers from my temple where I'd been knocked out.

I winced when he touched it.

"Trust me—if I could revive the men I killed for marring your face, I would. Just so that I could kill them again for hurting you."

I sat there in a state of shock, unable to say anything in return without fear of getting punished. Instead, I refocused my attention to my nephew and asked, "Did you take Naz too?"

He shook his head no. "Your nephew is safe. You're the only one who's not."

Relief washed over my senses for Naz. "I thought you weren't going to hurt me if I listened to you?"

"We both know that's not your true nature. You're a mafia princess, and your instinct will be to fight me. But don't you worry, pet. Trust me when I say that I look forward to breaking you down."

My body gave an involuntary shudder as he moved to stand in front of my face, giving me a perfect view of his erection. He palmed himself through his slacks.

"Like what you see?"

When I didn't answer fast enough, he roughly gripped onto my hair and yanked it back. I grimaced in pain, and more tears joined the others down my cheeks.

Unable to think from the discomfort, I blurted, "I don't!"

"You will," was all he said.

I was frozen, immobile again. He was close to me, closer than he had been before, and I could smell his scent. It was intoxicating. Consuming every last part of me.

He sat behind my back, straddling the piano bench. Then, in one quick, sudden motion, he laid my head on his shoulder, locking me in place by the forceful hold on my hair. I shut my eyes, not wanting him to see my terror.

It must have pissed him off because the next thing I heard was him ripping off my panties, and then…

Slap!

His hand struck my pussy, and my eyes snapped open. He didn't give me a chance to catch my bearings.

To recover.

To do anything but scream as loud as I could.

Slap!

Slap!

Slap!

I yelled so loud that my voice quickly became hoarse.

My lungs burned.

My chest ached.

My pussy throbbed.

And to show me how much he was truly enjoying this, he thrust his hard dick against my ass cheeks.

"Please…" I pleaded for mercy.

Slap!

Slap!

Slap!

"Please!" I wailed, loud enough to break glass.

I was covered in sweat, heat coursing its way through my core with emotions I didn't think were possible to feel in this fucked up situation I suddenly found myself in.

My chest seized.

My skin tingled.

My core pounded.

I didn't know if it was my begging or screaming that did him in, but he gradually let go of my hair and intimately began messaging my scalp. My head leaned into his caress, wanting the relief his hand was invoking on my tender head. I didn't want any part of the game he was playing, but my body's reaction to his touch proved that he had this power over me from the very beginning.

I turned my head to the side, away from him as hot tears streamed their way down the sides of my face.

It didn't end there.

He had only just begun to toy with me.

Suddenly, his fingers were softly rubbing where he'd just slapped me.

In comfort.

In pleasure.

In this twisted power struggle of how much he already owned me.

I moaned, even though I wanted to yell, even though I wanted to break down, even though I wanted to hate him with every ounce of my body.

His control.

His touch.

It was wreaking havoc on my entire being.

"Please..." I whispered, "Please..."

"Please what, pet?"

I didn't know what to say.

What to think.

My mind acted on its own, and I fought against his skilled fingers.

"No!" I screamed this time, louder than before.

He chuckled against my back, working my clit, knowing exactly how to touch my pussy.

"No!"

The bastard didn't let up, and my defiance only made him work harder. Simply proving that there was nothing he couldn't just steal from me if he wanted to.

Faster and harder, he manipulated me in this sick game of authority that I wanted to escape, but I was trapped in this room.

In his arms.

In his hands.

I tried to manage my emotions that were being solely governed by his voice, by his touch, by his erection that was still pressing into my ass.

"You're going to come for me, Juliet. And then you're going to thank me."

His words were fueled by my fire.

My restraint to prove him wrong.

But it was impossible.

He was too skilled.

Too precise.

Easily playing me like I played the piano.

Holding me tighter, firmer, never wanting me to feel anything other than what he desired. He roughly and determinedly moved his fingers, making me groan out in frustration and surrender. He was going to make me do it just to show me that he could.

My legs trembled.

My core locked up.

My eyes rolled to the back of my head.

I couldn't hold back any longer.

Resist it.

I saw stars as I came apart from the most intense orgasm I had ever felt.

"Good girl, Juliet," he praised me as much as he punished, and I knew it was just the beginning.

I laid there against him, immobile, lax, complacent.

"Now, hold still."

My body shuddered as he continued to mark me, cutting the ties of my hands.

When he was done, he once again stood in front of me before crouching to my level. For the first time, I could see him, really take a good look at him. His hair was dark and slicked back, emphasizing his chiseled cheekbones and five o'clock shadow. His broad shoulders and muscular chest were a few of the things I noticed as my gaze found the cross tattooed on his neck. That captured my attention the most, considering he was holding me hostage with a religious sacrament forever embedded onto his skin.

Bringing my attention back to his lips, he slid his wet fingers into his mouth and groaned in satisfaction.

My cheeks burned.

I was confused—both embarrassed and aroused.

Torn.

Sedated.

Was this his plan?

When he realized I appreciated his ruggedly handsome appearance, he grinned. It must have been my curious gaze that I couldn't hide from him. Not when he'd just stolen another part of me which he now owned as well.

With his stare narrowed in, he looked deep into my eyes and bit, "I won't love you. Ever." His jaw clenched. "Make no mistake, though, your days as Juliet Sinacore are finished. But your days as my pet have only just begun." He nodded toward the piano. Then ordered, "Play for me, Juliet, but first, where's my thank you for making you come?"

Instead of fighting for my emotions, my freedom, my hatred for him, I gave in to his request. "Thank you," I breathed out before turning to the piano.

Seeking refuge in music and not his wicked games.

CHAPTER TWO

Donovan

She did well. Better than I thought she would. After all this time, I finally had her. After four years of waiting for her, she was now a twenty-two-year-old woman.

A Sinacore.

I wanted her.

I had always, always wanted her.

Her innocence.

Her beauty.

Her body.

I'd been counting down the days to have her here with me. Away from everyone—her family, her friends—no one would find her. I made sure of it.

Images of Juliet flashed through my mind.

Her soft hair.

Her intoxicating scent.

Her sweet, salty pussy.

The way she cried.

Moaned.

Begged.

Mine.

Control wasn't given. Power wasn't handed. It was taken, exactly how I had taken her. My body relaxed, thinking about her in all the ways I shouldn't.

Slowly, I rose to my feet, adjusted my tie, and made my way out of my office. It was morning, the next day. Twenty-four hours since I had my first taste of her, and already I was craving more. Fully aware that nothing would ever be enough when it came to her.

It never was.

With each step, I felt more and more like myself. The grand hall of my mansion was empty, and its gold-plated ceiling seemed to glisten as I let myself in the room where Juliet would be waiting for me.

Two guards stood by the door.

"Open."

The guard jerked the heavy metal door to the side, and I walked in, nodding for them to close the steel door behind me. The entire room was blanketed in white, matching her complexion, but it was perfectly decorated with all the things she loved, including her beloved piano. *Or should I say mine?* I remembered the first time I had watched her play, in complete and utter awe of what she could do with her hands.

Her talent.

Her passion.

It poured out of her like the blood on my hands.

She was sleeping, passed out on a bed made for a queen. I watched her for most of the night from the cameras that were set up in her room. Even after I left her alone, she played the piano. Barely touching the food and water I had delivered to her. Each piece she played was darker, sadder, more intense than the last. Every emotion she felt was let out through the keys of black and white cords. It was all color. She was bright and bold. Fucking glowing from the inside out. Making my cock twitch at the sight of her. Images of me grabbing her by her sinful hips and fucking her up against the wall skated through my mind. Not to mention making her deep throat my dick between those perfect, pouty lips.

I tucked a piece of hair behind her ear and inhaled. She smelled like sunshine, rain, and life itself. Possessiveness washed over me as I pulled in every single emotion I had that was screaming at me to touch her more, to hug her.

Offer comfort when I had none to give.

Comfort was a lot like love—once you give it, there was no taking it back.

She would need it to survive, and then I'd fuck it out of her when it was convenient for me. I tried not to focus too much on the thought of her beneath me, blindfolded as I thrust into her.

The vision was too tempting.

I'd make her fall in love with me.

And in the end, if she didn't…

She'd die.

My eyes fluttered open, feeling him staring at me. He was sitting in a chair beside my bed.

Talk about fucking creepy.

As soon as my sleepy gaze connected with his, he ordered, "Strip," in a rough, demanding tone.

I didn't know what came over me; my father always said that my defiance would get the best of me one day.

Well, that day had come.

He simply stood, commanding respect and obedience. I didn't back down, lifting my chin higher and glaring at him. In one fluid motion, he unhooked the cufflinks of his collared button-down shirt and rolled up the sleeves. Through my stupidity, I still didn't cower. Instead, I sat up, tucking my knees under my body, and pretended like I wasn't scared as if I was a child. Unbuckling his belt next, he graciously pulled it out of the loops from his slacks. At first, I thought he was going to push himself on me. I could have been ready for that. Not once did I think he was going to do what he was about to.

With a snap of his belt in the air like a whip, I jumped. Instantly, I opened my mouth to tell him I would do what he ordered, but I was too late. He had other plans, and I only had myself to blame.

"You can't say I didn't warn you."

"What are you—"

He raised his hand and swung the belt down, right by my leg. I loudly gasped as it hissed through the air and then slapped against the mattress. My eyes widened with fear, immediately cowering away from him. Gripping the belt tighter, he whipped it again, by my ass this time. The sound echoed off the walls, and I shuddered, panting profusely.

"I'm sorry!" I shouted, hoping my apology would be enough to suffice him.

I was wrong; if anything…

It only provoked him.

His grasp white-knuckled the belt the whole time, not letting up on his assault. "Now, let's try this again. I. Said. Strip."

"Or you'll hit me?"

"Or you'll like it."

Just to prove that he would, he struck the belt to my ass, and it bit my skin. It didn't break my flesh, but I could feel my skin swelling. It was enough for me not to have to be told again, basically throwing off the clothes I was taken in. My naked body shook while my knees buckled, and my chest was rising and falling with each second that passed between us.

He didn't just look at me—he stared through me, seeing every last inch of me.

I swallowed the shame I felt, yet again, at my body's response to him. It wasn't the violence that got me; it was the look in his eyes that reminded me of all the men my father was always around.

Soulless.

"Happy now?!"

He moved so fast I barely had time to register that I was stumbling backward until his hand was on my neck, shoving me against the wall behind me. My mind pleaded with me to search for something sharp to stab him with, while my horror held me captive with his tight hold over my windpipe. This was when I noticed how tall he was; he towered over my small frame.

"I'd be happier if you obeyed my orders. That was me being kind to you, Juliet. Disobey me again and watch how fast you'll live to regret it."

With that, he cruelly let me go and nodded toward the bathroom. Once we were both standing in there, he turned on the shower, and I didn't have to be told this time. I stepped inside, only to be met with freezing cold water.

I shrieked and jolted back. "It's cold!"

"Of course it is." He leaned against the door, folding his arms over his solid chest. Relaxed as ever. "You get hot water when you deserve it."

I was naive to think he wouldn't punish me. "What happened to *you?*"

He stood, belt in hand, and the sound of it twisting between his fingers would be forever burned in my mind. "Did I say you could ask me questions, Juliet? Did I say you could even look at me?"

I clenched my jaw, shaking my head.

"Get your ass in the shower before I change my mind and teach you a lesson you won't soon forget."

I hesitantly stepped inside, shivering under the cold water, trying to ignore his words as I washed the horror from my body. I dug my soapy fingers into my skin and ignored the terror I felt building up in my soul. Squeezing my eyes shut, I prayed I could do this.

Live through this.

I started to think about my family. My life. The future I still desperately wanted to have that didn't include this sociopath. Until a scream erupted from my lips after his first lash, and then second, third, and fourth. He whipped my ass, the back of my thighs, my stomach, and my breasts.

"Please!" I dropped to my knees and begged.

Crying.

Frozen.

Fucking dying.

And then he was behind me, leaning forward, massaging the tender skin with his fingertips.

I hissed in pain. In agony. Trying so hard to not feel broken.

"You said you weren't going to hurt me unless I didn't listen to you. I listened! I was in the shower, wasn't I?" I'd never forget what he spewed next. It was now a part of me, embedded deep into my bleeding skin and becoming one with him.

Kissing my cheek, he confessed, "I couldn't resist watching you hurt for me."

CHAPTER THREE

Romeo

"Say it again. Slower this time."

I circled the beaten bodyguard and tried to keep myself from ripping his head from his shoulders with a fucking smile on my face.

Alessandro lowered his head with a wince. "It was fast, Romeo. Two men in all black, they looked like ours. It's all I saw."

I couldn't speak.

I simply reacted.

Throwing the first chair my hands could find against the wall, followed by another, and when everything was in chaos, my eyes fell to Alessandro, wondering if his head would split in two against the soundproof concrete room? Only one way to find out.

I charged toward him. He was the one who was supposed to be watching her, and they could have taken my son Naz too. They could have taken my wife, and my whole world would be in shambles.

Instead, they kidnapped my sister. Which was just as bad. He shouldn't be living; hell, he shouldn't even be fucking breathing.

"What do you think your punishment should be? For allowing Juliet Sinacore to slip from your grip and into someone's grasp? Huh? How should I fucking kill you?"

The only sounds that could be heard were his bones crunching, and his screaming filled my ears like a calming symphony. Only reminding me of my baby sister playing the piano for me.

His death wouldn't bring her back, but I didn't care. *Does that make me any different than the men who took Juliet?*

Blood splattered.

His last breath.

My eyes locked with his, so he would only see me in death.

In Hell.

Because let's fucking face it, that was where we were both going in the end.

Donovan

I trailed my fingers across the angry red skin of her flesh, gripping onto the belt in my left hand. I watched the way the water streamed down the blood on her skin and toward the drain making it disappear from her body. Whatever remaining human part of me that still existed was screaming in outrage, even though I was smiling.

I wanted her to fight me so bad it burned and ached inside of me.

"Do it, Juliet. I fucking dare you."

I could see it in her eyes—she wanted to try me. Her gaze shifted toward the belt in my hands before she stepped out of the shower, and I snapped the belt to her ankle. Not enough to draw blood, but to get my point across.

"You don't move unless I tell you to. Understood?"

Even her wet hair was tempting me as it draped down her breasts.

Jesus, she was breathtaking.

She nodded with tears still cascading down her flushed face, and I resisted the urge to fix the wounds I'd just inflicted. I would, but not now. The moment had come for me to start the process of truly making her mine in every sense of the word.

"Turn around."

Her vulnerability was almost too much for me to bear as she spun, following my orders. I stepped behind her while she faced the mirror. Grabbing the scissors from the pocket of my slacks, I skimmed the cool metal against her fair skin.

Her breathing caught, and with wide eyes, she watched in horror through the mirror as I ran the steel down her arm.

Across her chest.

Over her heart and then back up to her neck.

One of the first steps necessary in breaking her was getting rid of her old life and having her fit mine. In the way I saw her, wanted her, she belonged to me now, and I wouldn't stop until she fit my fantasy perfectly. I glided my fingers through her wet, heavy hair and then jerked it with my fist.

"Every woman wants to be you. Every man wants to fuck you."

Tears pooled in her eyes, and I forced her to look up at me. I cut the final thread in her mentally, emotionally, physically… With one snip, and then another, and another, a waterfall of tears poured down her cheeks while I battled the desire to lick them off her face with my tongue against her soft white skin.

Her hair fell from my fingers onto the ground, surrounding her in a broken halo. I hacked her dark hair until it was to her shoulders, holding up the last piece in front of her eyes so she could see how serious I was in who she belonged to.

"You hid from the world through your long, thick black hair, and I won't allow you to hide from me. Nothing between us, not even your luscious hair."

Her lips trembled, seeing herself in the mirror. The bruise on her temple, the lashes on her chest and stomach, along with her new haircut.

"Where's my tough girl, Juliet? Where did you she go?"

She didn't reply, and I could see she was going into shock.

"If you pass out, I'll only revive you and finish what I started. There's no escaping me, and the faster you realize that the easier this will be for you. Now, what do you say?"

Her mouth opened, and a strangled noise followed as she whispered, "Thank you."

"Now, say it like you mean it."

Fire flashed behind those tears. "Thank you," she firmly stated.

I leaned down and tenderly kissed her forehead. Then uttered, "You're welcome."

I choked on my tears of betrayal, bitterness building inside my soul until my heart felt like it was going to drown with it. I didn't recognize the woman staring back at me.

She was a stranger.

An imposter.

Lost.

My eyes shifted to his handsome, deceiving face through the mirror in front of us. I knew there was no place to run for cover.

Protection.

All I had was him.

The fucking villain.

And how pathetic was I that even through my tears of hopelessness, I still tried to turn to him for comfort—for sympathy, for anything really that would trick me into thinking this was a fairy tale when it was anything but that.

I was in his hell.

He wrapped his arms around my naked body, without morals, without rules, without a heart; he held me against his sturdy chest and allowed me to bawl my eyes out.

I was falling to the ground.
Fallen.
Gone.

And still—to my villain, I clung.

CHAPTER FOUR

Donovan

Everything about her was perfection, even with all the fallen pieces of her hair that stuck to my hands—I wanted her.

She was different.

This was different.

I knew it the moment I saw her for the first time. She was too pure, without the darkness like the sins I carried that had stained my soul. Oftentimes I wondered what it was like—walking around in this seedy world without the darkness looming and the heaviness dragging. It was my initial attraction to her as much as I didn't want to admit to it, but then again, nobody ever really does. Seeing something shiny, beautiful, untainted, I couldn't imagine anything more tempting than corrupting her, breaking her down to the barest of bare, stealing some of that goodness for myself, and then showing that same pretty little thing that the only reality that existed was the one you'd created for her.

A tear slid down her cheek, followed by another as she tried to crawl into herself, wrapping her arms around her knees like that would somehow protect her from my wrath. If anything, it attracted me even more, sending a bolt of lust through my body so strong I had a hard time exhaling.

I coaxed, "We're not finished yet," my voice heavy with desire.

She looked up at me through crystal blue eyes. "Why am I here?"

My smile was cruel, imagining the way I would lick those tears from her face, only to redden her body with my belt and create them all over again. Maybe I'd collect them, her tears, so I could stare at them in a glass bottle and remind myself and her that I controlled everything.

Even the number of tears that fell from her eyes.

"You're here"—I moved toward the door, waiting for the guards to open and hand me what I needed next—"because I want you to be here. It's really quite simple, pet."

"My father will never—"

"Let's leave your father out of this. You're here because I will it, just like you're alive because I want you to be. From here on out, you live for my pleasure only."

Her eyes flashed.

I hid my smile, and finally, the door opened with the guard giving me the bottle of dye. Her eyes widened when she realized what I was holding.

"Grab a towel."

"But—"

"This isn't a negotiation," I snapped. "Grab a fucking towel, kneel in front of the bathtub with your head bowed, and wait for me."

She looked ready to murder me. Good, I loved it when they fought. Sometimes, too much.

At my words, she slowly got to her feet. Her hands shook, whether in fear or something else; I didn't know and really didn't fucking care. Eventually, she'd crave me in unfathomable and unforgivable ways. Her lean legs carried her into the bathroom, and I watched in anticipation as she knelt in front of the bathtub, her knees on the towel, her short dark hair in a tattered mess below her ears.

I'd allow her to fix it later. For now, I needed something.

Desperately.

I waited longer than ten minutes, testing her to see if she'd rebel, talk back to me, or even stand up thinking I'd forgotten about her. Still, she knelt. She'd be sore from sitting in that position. Meaning she'd welcome the reprieve when I allowed her to stand; she'd thank me and hate me at the same time.

A little bit of pleasure.

A little bit of pain.

They go hand in hand when turning someone into a pet for a collector—only this time, I was training her for me. Not for anyone else.

Just me.

I leaned over her and turned on the faucet. Once it was ice cold, I shoved her head underneath the water with one hand and disclosed, "I prefer blondes."

Water sputtered out of her mouth from cascading down her face.

"You like this," I simply stated, gripping her by the hair as her nipples hardened. "Even if your mind refuses to give up the control, your body craves the comfort of pain; want to know why, Juliet?"

"No." She clenched her teeth. "You're a monster."

"I try." I grinned down at her chest. "I wonder if you're as wet between your thighs…"

Captives always tried to appear strong—most of them broke before they even realized what was happening, and she'd be no different.

"Bow your head," I instructed.

She slowly did as I asked. I shook the bottle before spilling it over her roots, using my hands to pull the color down the short length of her hair. Something about seeing her bent over in submission, something about her flawless tears as I erased her identity had me so turned on I couldn't fucking think straight.

"Why?" she asked again.

I stared her down, unable to actually get the words out without sounding fucking weak. I saw you and knew I'd have to kidnap, claim, fuck, and heal you.

The memory of the last pet I had and trained for another man quickly appeared through my mind.

"He's waiting for you at the end of the hall."

A tear slid down her cheek. "At least tell me you got a good price for me, Donovan."

I shrugged. "You weren't a virgin, but the price was still fair."

"Did you ever," she screamed. "Did you ever even love me?"

This wasn't the first or last time a pet would fall in love with me. It was just part of the process. I ignored her questions.

Her lips trembled. "It was real, all of it; I know it."

I shook my head slowly and leaned forward, pushing off the doorframe.

"It was all to train you for another man, someone better; you'll see. You may have been mine, but, Catarina, I was never yours. Understand?"

She looked ready to throw her body at me. "You're, you're—"

"I was never your master, which is why you don't address me as such. Your owner is waiting for you, and I wouldn't keep him waiting, pet. The last thing you want to do is show him you have no training. I won't punish you, but he will. My job here is done now."

"I hate you! Do you hear me? I fucking hate you!"

I hated myself too sometimes, however, not for the same reasons. No, I hated myself because I needed the violence in order to experience a sliver of love. After all, that was what happened when you grew up locked in closets and watching your mother die right before your eyes by a man who was supposed to love her. My father. In the end, I killed him too. Not for her; I did that for no one but me.

You see, the true monsters of the world were the ones that hid in plain sight like saviors when they were nothing but sinners in broad daylight.

I shook away the memory. "Keep this on for twenty minutes. I'll set a timer."

"Where are you going?" A panicked expression crossed her exotic features.

With a smirk, I palmed the front of my pants and showed her what she did to me.

"Unless you want me to fuck you right now, I suggest you let me leave."

She barked out a bitter laugh. "Oh, now you care about what I want?"

"Careful, pet. You don't want to continue speaking to me like you have a right to, or else I'll have to remind you again why you don't. Are we clear?"

"You're just imagining all the ways you'd love to make me cry, make me fight, make me hate you. I bet that's why you're hard just thinking about it."

I almost groaned in pleasure then realized what she was doing. She was playing with fire. How fucking adorable. Leaning down, I tilted her chin up toward me.

"One day, you'll be on your knees begging for my touch, my tongue, my cock."

She jerked away. "Doubtful."

I smiled, despite wanting to take her over my knee. Pressing my lips against her shoulder while my right hand snaked around her neck, I squeezed.

"Since you're so fucking adamant on having me punish you, then touch me, Juliet."

"No!"

I gripped harder. "Touch me." I grit my teeth. "Feel what you do to me."

"You're a disgusting, miserable human!" Her eyes flashed in an invitation I couldn't resist.

With a wicked grin, I jerked her chin between my fingers and whispered, "I'll allow your disrespect this one time, but don't think I'm not keeping score. Next time, I'll beat the disrespect right out of you. And trust me, pet." I didn't hesitate. "I'd much prefer it that way too."

Juliet

I wanted to be my own hero. My own savior. The woman I was raised to be.

Brave.

Strong.

Intelligent.

Instead, all I kept thinking about was how my cruel captor smiled at me, like he knew a secret I didn't, like he knew me better than I knew myself, which was frankly terrifying.

Something in his gaze felt familiar, but the more I stared, the more I was sucked beneath his monstrous spell.

I couldn't break.

I had to stay strong, especially when it came to his full lips and angry comments. "Who hurt you? Who made you this way?" But I figured he wouldn't tell me even if I held him at gunpoint.

The dye was starting to make my scalp itch as I stayed on my knees on the towel, staring at the plain white ceramic tile, wondering how the hell I got on this man's radar. Clearly, I wasn't some ransom. I had so many questions but knew asking them would either get me further punishment or him further aroused. Either way, I was screwed.

My tears dried up out of necessity. He seemed to like it when I cried, so I made myself a promise that I wouldn't anymore, that I'd stare straight ahead and do what he said until I could escape. Until I could free myself from him or kill him. Whatever came first. Minutes passed as I wondered if he truly was touching himself. When the sick bastard returned to the bathroom, he was the vision of serenity, controlled, neutral.

I didn't know which one was worse, his calm or his storm…

"Bend," he muttered so low I nearly missed it as he gently held my head beneath the faucet and washed the dye from my short hair.

My stomach sank, looking down at the drain. My old life was being washed away, and my captor was holding me like it was a comfort when it was everything short of a nightmare.

I immediately tensed.

"They may as well be your sins, Juliet…"

His breath was hot on my face, his lips touching my ear with little zaps of pleasure that made me hate myself.

"Look at the old you being washed right away, and imagine how much more empowered you'll be now that you know who you are."

"I've always known who I am," I said through a clenched jaw.

"No." He ran a finger down the back of my neck. "You were in a cage… I just set you free."

I had nothing to say to that other than he was a sociopath and a liar.

"I was happy."

"You weren't." He continued caressing the back of my neck with one finger. "I saw you first when you were eighteen. You were playing a concert for a very well-known family in the greater Seattle area. It was Christmas, and you wore a red dress. Every man in that auditorium was pulled under a spell only someone as talented and beautiful as you can create, myself included. You left your heart on that stage, on those piano keys, and I swore to myself I'd never let you be that vulnerable again unless you were by my side. Your father looked right through me that night, and I went home clutching the program with one hand and touching myself with the other, imagining your soft curves, the ruby red lips that matched your dress—you were mine before you even knew it. And now you're mine for good."

I felt ready to puke, swaying on my knees. "If that's who you fell for, then why change me?"

"Such a simple question." He pulled me to my feet. "Such a complicated answer. You weren't allowed to dye your hair, were you?"

I gasped. "There is no way you could possibly know—"

"You wanted to cut it at one point, just like you wanted to take ballet lessons, just like you wanted to play the piano professionally. You see me as a monster, putting you on a pretty shelf. I see myself as the one man who knows how to let you be."

He pulled me back against him, his lips on my neck. "I can't wait for the day when you look up at me with those gorgeous eyes and say thank you. And truly fucking mean it. Not just because you think I'll beat your ass if you don't ... which I will."

I would not cry.

I would not give in.

I simply froze while he held me, wondering why my heart was beating so fast.

"You'll see. I'm never wrong, especially when it comes to you."

I bowed my head. "You don't even know me," I whispered under my breath.

He grabbed my chin, making me look up at him.

Smiling, he argued, "I know how to make you come. The rest is irrelevant for now."

CHAPTER FIVE

Juliet

"Get on the bed."

He sensed my apprehension.

"Juliet…" he cautioned before I slowly walked toward the mattress and sat on the edge.

"Remove the towel."

I peeked up at him through my lashes to find his eyes still remained dark and callous. Throwing the towel at his feet, he smirked at my attempt to be rebellious. His Adam's apple moved, walking over to me, each footstep deliberately calculated and precise. He kneeled down to my level, sitting on the soles of his shoes before grabbing my chin, settling it to look directly at him.

"Spread your legs, pet."

"What?" I asked in confusion, sheer terror, my voice caught in my throat almost like my body was rebelling against his demands.

"You heard me."

"I-I-I-I…"

"I-I-I…" he mocked in an agitated tone, both infuriating me and making me want to cry.

"Why must you defy me? That pride of yours isn't doing anything other than making me hurt you. But maybe that what's you what … for me to hurt you?"

I fervently shook my head; he was insane. "That's absurd. Why would I want you to hurt me?"

"Then prove me wrong, Juliet. Be a good girl and spread your legs for me. Unless you want me to force you?"

When I didn't move fast enough, he slapped my thigh. There would be a handprint where he'd struck me, I knew it—like he was marking me everywhere.

"Now!"

I jumped, shaking. "Please…"

"Please what, pet?"

"Please don't make me do this."

"You're sadly mistaken if you think for one second that I care about what you want. You either spread your legs for me, or I'll spread them for you. The choice is once again yours. Choose wisely because, with the way I'm feeling, I'll have no mercy on you."

"Why are you doing this to me? What do you want? Is it money?"

He scoffed out a snide chuckle, letting go of my chin to lean back and sit on the balls of his feet.

"Take a good look around. Does it look like I need money?"

"Then what is it? I don't understand. Just please make me understand. You at least owe me that."

He narrowed his devious eyes at me, making me shiver from the expression on his face. I was fully aware I was pushing his limits, but I couldn't help it. I was a fucking Sinacore. It was in my blood. It was how I was made. I wasn't used to cowering down to anyone. My family would be so unbelievably disappointed in me. The shame of just thinking about what my father and brother would say seeing me like this…

Naked on a bed.

With a sadistic son of a bitch ordering me to spread my legs.

I could never tell them.

But I could at least know in my soul that I fought, that I tried to become more than the monster in front of me, that while he was making demands, confusing me, dominating me, I could make my own plans— revenge.

"I don't owe you one damn thing, pet. It's best if you recognize that."

I wanted to scream.

Fight.

Kill him.

Not one part of me wanted to spread my legs for his amusement.

"If I do, then what? What happens after that?"

He probably knew I was buying time, but it was all I had. My questions, and it was, unfortunately, the one thing that truly pissed him off.

"Spread your fucking legs, and you'll find out."

This was where I truly lost my shit. I had nothing left to lose, nothing to gain.

"Fuck you!"

He growled from deep within his chest and lunged at me.

Instantly, I shouted, "I'm sorry!"

It didn't matter. I knew it wouldn't. Although, it didn't stop me from repeating it over and over like a mantra, "I'm sorry! I'm sorry! I'm sorry!"

He roughly shoved me back onto the bed with his hand over my neck. I thought he was going to choke me, hit me, hurt me in ways I never thought possible.

I wasn't wrong.

He was going to hurt me, just not in the way I imagined.

My hands instinctively went to his sharp hold over my neck.

"Please! I'm sorry! I'm so fucking sorry!"

"You aren't"—he leaned forward close to my ear—"but you will be."

Locking me in place with his tight, crippling grip, he slapped my pussy so fucking hard that my legs just spread open for him. I shut my eyes, not wanting to see what he was going to do next.

"Look at me!"

"No!"

"I said fucking look at me!"

"No!"

He didn't waver, cupping his hand over my mouth and nose; I couldn't breathe. Instinctively, I kicked my legs which only made him straddle my body. I thrashed around, at least I tried to, but I was losing air. My oxygen was depleting, and it didn't help that I was wasting it pitifully trying to fight him off.

I was going to pass out, and at this point, I didn't give a shit. It meant I didn't have to look at him, hear him, want to kill him for however long I was out.

Everything started going dark.

Darker.

Black.

Complete and utter opaqueness. Until the only thing I could see was my life playing out for me like a tragic Shakespearian play. I saw it all, starting from when I was little. I went from being with my captor, with his hands around my neck, to being home.

Safe and sound.

Happy.

Loved.

At first, I thought I was dreaming. My head felt heavy, and my body even heavier; the room felt like it was spinning. I was lightheaded, and even though I had just woken up from fainting, I was tired, exhausted even. I slowly moved my head side-to-side, trying to wake up. Only then did I realize there was something on my eyes, keeping me from being able to see or open them.

I should've felt fear, but I was drained of any emotion. I allowed it to take over and passed out again. The next time I woke up, I was less hazed, recognizing instantly that my displacement had not changed. I was in the exact same position I was in before.

Except this time, there was what felt like a rope tied around my wrists and ankles, binding my arms to the headboard, and my legs were spread apart, knotted by rope to the bedposts. I couldn't close them. I wanted to yell, but it came out as a muffled shriek. Nobody was going to rescue me but me, and I couldn't even get out of the damn ropes or stay awake long enough to scream. Not that it mattered.

I remembered a psych class, where the professor did an entire lecture on fear and how it motivated people, how it was one of the only things that could create a perfect world, and I remembered hating that it made sense, that it sounded right. Not everything was fueled by adrenaline, fed by fear, and there was nothing I could do about the way I responded, even when I told myself to calm down, to think, to negotiate. I felt myself constantly defaulting , protecting myself.

I tried to move until my skin felt raw, fighting until my body couldn't move anymore, and I was sweating profusely. I should have been crying, and I couldn't tell if I was in shock because I didn't feel anything.

I was numb.

It was only then that I felt the back of a hand touch the side of my face, and I froze, not moving one muscle. My mind went into overload...

"Is it you?" I asked, my voice trembling. Thinking it could be someone else—I was unsure of which would be better or worse. Him or someone new...

As if reading my mind, he countered, "Do you want it to be?"

I breathed out a sigh of relief. His hand was still on the side of my face and hadn't moved. It was comforting and creepy all at the same time. My breathing was labored, and my heart was racing. More questions started to arise in my mind.

Before I could continue with my mindless thoughts, he asked, "Are you done with your temper tantrum?"

I swallowed hard. "Yes."

"Good girl."

Rat bastard and his demeaning praise.

"Can you please take the blindfold off?" I tried again, voice easy, all traces of the tremble gone.

"Seeing as you wouldn't look me in the eyes before, I assumed you wanted to stay in your self-preservation of darkness."

"I don't want to anymore."

"How convenient," he snapped.

"Please. I won't fight you again."

"You're tied to your bed, pet. You can't do much of anything right now."

I whimpered, wanting to see.

"You really do have a pretty pussy, Juliet," he laughed at me, stripping away the last bit of my dignity. "It's just the right shade of pink."

I sucked in air from the fresh tears coming out of my eyes. I'd never in my life felt lower, more demeaned, embarrassed, afraid, and yet I responded; I physically responded like someone sick in the head.

"Pet … when someone pays you a compliment, you should say thank you. Where the fuck are your manners? I bathe you, I give you water, food, shelter, and now, I tell you that your cunt is pretty, and what do you say?" he taunted, hitting something hard against the soles of my feet.

I whimpered again.

Was that a cane?

He did it a couple more times.

"Thank you, thank you, thank you!" I shouted, appeasing him while still trying to keep my fight on the inside. I had to escape, and if that meant I thanked him for his insanity, then so be it.

"Much better. We're going to have to work on those manners and respect, pet. I won't have you disrespecting me."

"What are you going to do to me?" I questioned again. *How many times would we have this conversation? And how many times would I be punished for the truth?*

"Whatever the fuck I want."

"Can you tell me your name?"

"You earn the right to know my name, Juliet. And we both know how much of a bad girl you've been. You disappoint me."

"I'm sorry," was the only thing I could reply that would simply appease him.

"Look what my punishment has done for your manners; this is the politest you've been since you arrived."

"Can you please just tell me your name?"

"Don't be so needy, pet. I don't like it."

I sniffled, just wanting something for myself. Anything. At this point, I'd probably beg on my hands and knees just to know his initials.

"Why do you think you deserve to know my name? Do you think you're going to refer to me by it?"

"What do you mean?"

"I'm done answering your questions."

"You haven't answered a single one."

"You will refer to me as Master. There. Now you know my name."

What. The. Fuck.

"Am I being trafficked? Is that what this is about? Are you training me to sell me?"

"No. I'm breaking you for me."

His answer made my heart slow down.

"Is that what you want? To break me?"

I would never forget the next thing that flew out of his mouth.

"You'll soon find out."

In the following weeks, I learned a lot about myself.

Especially how right he was.

CHAPTER SIX

Three Days Later

Whatever I thought was a breakthrough with me thanking my captor turned into my worst nightmare. He untied me and left me alone. Naked. For two whole days, I didn't see him, feel him, hear him. Nothing. It was like he disappeared, leaving me only with my questions and fear. I was starving, living off of water I drank from the faucet in the bathroom. I refused to give him the satisfaction he craved. Until I couldn't take it anymore. The lack of food and being locked in this room was making me feel as if I was going insane.

I snapped, needing him like he said I would.

Looking straight into the camera in the corner of my room, I yelled, "Please, Master. I'm hungry!"

I hated that I sounded so weak when I wanted to feel strong. I hated that I gave him what he sought; calling this bastard Master was one of the hardest things I'd ever done. Minutes later, the door opened with a tray that looked like it had bread and soup on it. I swear I almost dropped to my knees to thank him.

He grinned. "Was that so hard, pet?"

I resisted the urge to tell him it was. Instead, I shook my head.

"Your food is earned when you have manners." He walked toward me and sat in the chair beside my bed. Nodding to the floor, he demanded, "Crawl to me."

I stumbled back from the impact of his order.

"Once you crawl to me, you'll sit on the floor beside my feet with your hands behind your back, bowing your head in submission. You'll wait until I feed you from my hand. Understood?"

My stomach grumbled.

"Understood, pet? Or would you like to continue to starve?"

Slowly, I dropped to my knees.

"Good girl."

Little by little, I crawled my way toward him while tears fell out of my eyes. I did what he wanted, feeling like nothing but a fucking dog, not a dog, a pet.

His pet.

I waited.

His thumb lifted my chin to look into his seedy stare. "So pretty for a pet, now what do you say when I give you a compliment, and I'm going to feed you, Juliet?"

My entire body shook as I whispered, "T-thank you."

"Good, girl. Very good girl."

The second I felt his fingers in my mouth, I swallowed the bread without taking a bite first. It hurt all the way down my throat and chest, but at least...

I was fed.

CHAPTER SEVEN

One Week Later

"Wake up!" Master yelled, jolting me out of a restless sleep.

I was still naked, angry, and tired. It must have been the middle of the night. He was shirtless, his golden skin exposed for me to bask in. Gorgeous muscles framed his shoulders; his abs were a thing of beauty. However, the vision of him had me realizing that not all pretty things were meant to be touched, to be admired. Maybe some of the prettiest of all should come with warning signs.

"Yes, Master," I mumbled.

"On your knees."

Cautiously, I moved from the bed to my knees and waited. He pressed his hand against my back and shoved me closer to the floor until my legs hurt until my face was pressed sideways against the floor.

"Let's try this again."

I couldn't speak. My jaw hurt as I waited for the pain to end. For the nightmare to be over.

For my bedroom.

My family.

My friends.

My safety.

No matter how attractive he was—he would always be the monster.

He jerked his hand away, and I heard him shuffling around.

"Lift your head."

Slowly, I did.

"Now, crawl to me and come lay next to me."

"Lay next to you?"

"Did I ask for questions, pet?"

I wanted to scream but screaming meant I'd be punished, and I was just too fucking exhausted. Over the last week, he only came into my room to feed me from his hand. Three times a day, making me look forward to his company and the comfort of the food he always brought with him. Each time, we played this same game.

Master.

Pet.

He talked about random things, praising and complimenting me on my manners. Telling me how much of a good girl I was for him. It was sick and fucking demented; he made me need him. To think about only him. When he would be back, when he would be with me again, when he would feed me, touch me, tell me how beautiful I was.

Surrendering.

Complacent.

Broken.

"I'm sorry, Master."

"Good girl."

Those two words, those two fucking words, I looked forward to them too. Getting on my hands and knees, I did as I was told. The instant I sat beside him, he didn't hesitate in the least. Laying my head on his chest. I think I froze for a few seconds.

"Relax, pet, and go back to sleep."

There was something about the way those words just effortlessly flowed from his mouth that was calming, peaceful, so I shut my eyes. When I woke up later, I was alone. He was gone, and I instantly missed his warmth against my skin, his heartbeat against my ear, his body against mine.

Further reminding me, I truly was his.

CHAPTER EIGHT

Juliet

Two Weeks Later

I was used to it now. The loneliness, the way it wrapped itself around me like the blanket that was on my bed. I was used to him now, the smug wicked looks from my master. The way he stared at my body like he wanted to eat me alive, only to kill me later. He was the only human contact I had, the only voice I heard, the only…

The only…

The only…

The list was endless, and I felt so weak, needing him, depending on him, missing him as if he were my lover and not my villain in this reality of what my life had become. I craved every last single thing about him—from his company, to his hands, to his body, to his masculine scent and his words. There wasn't a part of me that didn't yearn for him. I knew it was sick; it was the only way I could survive this imprisonment. In this golden cage, he captured me in. It was all part of his sinister plan, succeeding in what he threatened, what he promised, what he knew would happen in the end.

I was ashamed, humiliated, broken.

And yet, I still longed for him in ways I never thought possible. Wiping the tears away from my cheeks, I waited for the inevitable. He walked in.

Two steps.

Four.

Ten.

He was sitting on the chair by my bed, and like a perfect pet, I crawled to him. Except this time, I laid my head on his lap, wanting something more. He didn't punish me for not submitting; understanding my silent plea, he rubbed my head so gently.

For the first time in what felt like an eternity, I smiled. Seeking refuge in his storm.

CHAPTER NINE

Two Weeks Later

The door opened.

His smile returned, but this time it looked almost hopeful as he took five steps into the room, shut the door, and made his way over to the bed I was laying in. It was late; I was starting to fall asleep. I wasn't a good girl the day before, and all day today, I was tied to the bed, spread-eagle again. My punishment for throwing a temper tantrum was that he wouldn't allow me to wear any clothes, and I was over being naked.

He turned a full-on smile against me like a weapon.

"I'm going to touch you now."

My head hung to the side. I didn't have the strength or ability to hold it up any longer as I laid there, waiting for the worst. I shuddered when I felt his hand caress the top of my mound. He was gentle and tender, smoothly running his fingers up and down. My breathing elevated, and I couldn't control the tears, the confusion that was pouring out of my shaken body.

It was when I started to cry.

Break down.

Fall apart.

"Shhh…" he whispered.

At first, I thought I imagined it, but then I heard it again. "Shhh…"

It was low and vibrant.

"Shhh…"

That sound would forever be embedded in my mind. I didn't dare say another word. The simple yet powerful sound of what he was implying burrowed deep among my bones and made itself a home. His hand continued to caress me in a back and forth motion. I wanted to defy or say something, but I wasn't ready for the repercussions.

Within moments, I felt him start rubbing cream on the wounds of my wrists and ankles from being tied up all day. I hissed at the cool feeling against my open flesh.

"It's cold cream. It will help you heal faster."

More tears fell from my eyes. I couldn't keep up with all the emotions coursing through me.

I hated him, though, I wanted his comfort, and I appreciated his kindness in this moment. He was the one who inflicted the pain on me in the first place, but it was because I was defiant and asked for clothing when he wanted me naked.

I made him hurt me, right?

Once he was done, he ran a cold compress against my face and then my whole body. It was refreshing, comforting, soothing, and I didn't want it to end. It provided this false sense of reassurance, even if it was only for a few minutes. I let myself think that everything was going to be okay. He left the washcloth on my stomach, and water began to drip to my lips.

"It's just water. You're dehydrated."

It dripped onto my lips, and I took as much of it into my mouth as possible. I was starving for it, and at that point, I realized that I had no say in what would happen, and I needed to follow instructions. The dehydration was apparent; he was right about that. I didn't care that it was getting all over my upper body and the mattress behind me. I took in every ounce of what he was giving, completely greedy for it. When the water stopped, I closed my mouth to enjoy the moisture that replaced the dryness. I waited for his next word, his next move. My heart raced, and hysteria threatened to resurface while he simply brushed my wet hair away from my face.

I was covered in sweat, and the heat coursing its way through my body made it apparent how badly I wanted him to touch me. I could feel my nipples harden and my skin tingle as he stared at me, and he knew what I felt and what he was doing to me. I didn't want any part of it, but my body's reaction to his touch proved that he always had power over me. Now more than ever before.

I would never get over this, I would never be normal again, and I would never trust my instincts again after the way I was feeling from one simple drop of water, to one slow caress across my face. I craved any sort of human connection—no, I craved humanity amidst his depravity.

His grip tightened around my wrist, massaging it, trying to relieve my discomfort. I turned my head to the side, away from him. Not wanting him to see the effect he had over me.

"You can't hide from me, pet."

His forefinger and thumb rubbed at the most sensitive part of where the bindings were cutting, and I moaned. Even though I couldn't see his face, I knew he was smiling. He was enjoying what he was doing to me, and I hated him for it.

"Thank you," I said without him demanding it.

I knew he was fighting some internal battle with himself, his demons, and I was suddenly one of them. He repeated the same process on my other wrist and ankles before he fed me warm oatmeal. Once I was done eating, there was an eeriness in the room. It was thick and heavy.

I smiled, despite myself.

However, it was quickly replaced when he spewed, "I'll untie you after I make sure you're still a virgin."

I stopped smiling, and before I could make a peep, his fingers started rubbing my clit with precise determination.

I sucked in a breath. This was the first time he was touching me like this since the first day I'd arrived. Faster and faster, his skilled fingers had my body shaking.

"Ahhh..." I panted, feeling the ecstasy he was delivering.

His other hand found the inside of my mouth, pushing his fingers as far as they would go down my throat, causing me to gag at the intrusion. He did it a few times, and each time the gagging became louder and heavier. He pushed them in one last time and pulled them out with a trail of my spit following behind, placing it all over my pussy.

My eyes watered, and I hacked and coughed, but that didn't stop my body from responding to his touch. The more pressure he applied to my clit, the closer I got to release. I felt his hard cock on my leg through his slacks.

"You want to come?"

"Yes…" I shamelessly begged.

He slapped my pussy a few more times, and that was all it took for me to shake with a deep, steady release. My come dripped down my inner thighs and all over his fingers, and he didn't stop until every last drop was out of me. My head swirled with aftershocks, and that was when he slid his fingers inside of me. It was the first time a man had ever done so, and I squirmed at the discomfort. It hurt a lot, and it was only his fingers that were inside of me.

"And right there, pet …" he rasped in a husky, addicting tone. "You feel that? It's your virginity. Now the real question is, should I claim it with my fingers or with my cock instead?"

"Please," I pleaded, for I didn't know what.

I was embarrassed, ashamed, afraid, and I still wanted him, needed his touch.

He growled from deep within his chest.

It was over before it even began. He removed his fingers and licked them clean. Backing away, he walked toward the door.

"Aren't you going to untie me?"

"When you're my good girl, you get to sleep in my arms; until then, you get nothing but darkness while you're bound to the bed."

He turned off the light, and once I heard the door being locked, I welcomed the sleep with open arms, allowing myself to slip back into dreams of my old life where I wasn't being held captive.

My dreams turned into nightmares, and somewhere along the night, I was screaming in terror. Only to be told, "Shhh… shhh… shhh…"

I passed out again, only this time I wasn't tied up.

No more dreams.

No more nightmares.
I was at peace.

Laying there, wrapped in my villain's arms.

CHAPTER TEN

Donovan

"**F**uck!"

I kicked the door, again and again, my foot banging against the metal until I felt nothing. When I was feeling everything. She was sleeping in my arms. It was too soon, but I couldn't fucking help myself. She was hysterical, having a nightmare more than likely about me. I wanted her fear, yet it needed to be on my terms. Not hers. I watched Juliet from the monitor in my office for as long as I could bear it.

"You done yet?" a familiar voice questioned down the corridor.

I didn't turn around.

I didn't have to.

"Does it look like I'm done?" I kicked it again.

I sent the guards to go play fetch while I tended to my property.

That's all she is, Donovan. You're just taking care of what's yours—nothing more, nothing less.

"I can smell her fear."

"What?" I spun around. "You a werewolf now, Troy?"

"I don't like blood as much as you do. You sure you still want this one? I could take her off your hands ... break her for you, really challenge her to become the best version of herself. You know how it goes, kill all hope, burn down everything, so she becomes reliant on you. It's like having a gorgeous slave who would kill just for your approval."

I clenched my fists and finally gave him my full attention. Troy was my father's best friend, and in some form, he was a father figure to me as well—taking me under his wing after I had killed my father. He was one of the only people who understood me, understood what we did, what we provided, and was the only one capable of seeing past every one of my cold, calculated looks to the man inside of me.

And sometimes, I hated him for it.

Troy wasn't intimidated or threatened by my presence and made sure to put me in my place every chance he'd get. It didn't happen often. He was getting older and didn't have the power he once had.

Especially, over me.

"What do you really want?" I changed the subject, walking into another room that stored all my liquor. I poured a dram of whiskey into my favorite glass. "You never visit when I'm working."

"I missed you," he chuckled, sitting in his usual spot. The black leather chair was his favorite.

Our habits kept us focused, and each of us were religiously tied to everything we did when breaking someone new, down to the very clothes we wore and people we talked to.

This lifestyle wasn't simple. It was a calculated web of desire, deceit, lust, training, approval, and money.

And I fucking loved it.

Most days.

He wore a black suit with his black shirt; the first two buttons were undone, revealing the matching tattoo we both got when we started our company. Something I couldn't think about now, not with his arrogant blue eyes practically twinkling with amusement and not with his dark blond hair pulled away from his face like he'd constantly been running his hands through it. Plotting, thinking, planning. Even in his sixties, he was striking. According to almost every woman he had trained.

In the back of my mind, I was reminded of that day.

The day my world went dark.

The day he offered to rescue me, and I hated that he was right to this very day. My father's best friend, now my business partner and the only man I could trust.

But could I really trust him?

Fuck no.

We were slave trainers. Sometimes the women were trafficked, and sometimes they were just taken. I took my seat, leaning back, folding my hands in my lap, and waiting for the question I knew would come. It was inevitable. After all, he always wanted what he couldn't have, and I typically always gave him what was out of his reach. I was indulgent like that, and it was the only way we really showed affection.

Gifts.

Of the female variety.

A lot of them.

He uncorked the wine, poured a half glass, and lifted it to his lips with a superior smirk before saying, "How much?"

I knew it was coming. He was always so fucking predictable.

The question itself wasn't shocking at all; my reaction, however, was.

Stomach clenched, I took a calming breath and shrugged. "More than you can afford."

"Impossible."

"Is it, though?"

"Donovan…" He shook his head. "You know I'm good for it, so answer the damn question before you ruin my night—is this Castella wine?"

"Vintage," I answered in a clipped tone. "Wasted on a bastard like you."

"Cheers." He winked. "And try not to sound so threatened, D. This is business, not pleasure."

I flinched at that.

"Or is it pleasure? Is this … more than just a business arrangement? Is that why you've been with her longer than usual?" He set his glass down, then cracked his knuckles and stood. "I called earlier; your assistant said you were busy, so I assumed work. I came by twice, and both times you were busy. With *her*. We both know it takes a few hours tops. You leave, you come back, you leave, you fuck with their heads, and then you have the best product possible, but you…" He pointed, his smile firmly in place. "It hasn't been a few hours, Donovan. I even heard you grabbed the cold cream."

I scowled. "Every pet is different. You should know that. Oh wait…" I snapped my fingers. "You wouldn't since you accidentally killed—"

"Shut the hell up," he yelled. "We won't speak of it. Ever."

I shrugged, knowing I'd hit one of his buttons. "Whatever you say, Troy."

His eyes narrowed. "Just admit that you're keeping her or offer her up for sale. Your choice."

"Nice." I laughed mockingly. "Has anyone ever told you that your manipulation schemes need more polish?" I stood and stared out the large bay window as lights filled the night sky. "I won't give her up today."

"What about tomorrow?"

"What about next week?" I sighed. "It doesn't matter because she's one to keep."

"Because last time that worked out so well for your fat—"

"We all have our things we don't talk about, Troy. Don't make me fucking kill you. I'm wearing my favorite tie."

Footsteps sounded. "This isn't over, D. I'll be back. Don't underestimate my love for you. Or my need to possess something dear to you. It didn't go well last time and won't go well this time. Remember how the game works… In the end, the ones you care for suffer."

"And who'd you pick this time?"

"Like you don't know."

"Twenty-seven, blue eyes, reddish-brown hair, has a dimple on her right cheek, father owns two shipping companies, one little brother, married, one older sister, divorced, drives a Maserati and just can't stop waiting for her prince to come, does that sound about right?"

He started slowly clapping. "So you did your research."

"You have yours. I have mine. Why the question, Troy? Truly?"

He was silent for a few seconds. "Maybe I'm just greedy."

I laughed. "There is no maybe, Troy. You are a greedy fuck. I'm warning you now—back off. This one's…" I refused to say different. Instead, I shrugged then glared. "Mine to break."

"If you can," he said hauntingly. "If you can. She's been with you how many weeks now? Over a month, right?"

A shiver ran down my spine as I watched him leave, like a foreboding sensation of dread and fear wasn't something I was used to feeling.

Until her.

Until now.

Until my Juliet.

Fuck me.

My achy wrists were now tied up again; the ugly pieces of rope were cutting into my skin, marring me, provoking me, and worst of all, reminding me of whose I was.

And what he would eventually do.

I clenched my legs together or at least tried to. They were both tied up as well.

Why?

He undid the ties, and I slept in his arms. Why, even when he was cruel, I wanted his name to fall from my lips, so even if I cursed him to hell, I knew whose name I was screaming? The blindfold had fallen down toward my nose while a fire roared in the corner, and blackness overtook the rest of my surroundings. Maybe on purpose, maybe because my villain thrived in the dark. Whatever it was, I was at least alone, able to breathe, to think.

Suddenly, the door opened, and I stilled as footsteps sounded.

A voice I didn't recognize whispered in my ear, "One day, you'll know what it's like to serve at my mercy. Today. Is not that day."

He left me shaking until the door opened again what felt like hours later. I tensed, assuming it was the terrifying stranger only to have the blindfold pulled from my face and my villain's dark eyes searching mine.

"Where?"

"What?"

"Where!" he demanded an answer.

I didn't understand. "What? What!" I tried to scramble back as he grabbed my wrists and stared at them, his eyes roaming from the rope toward my face, down my body, and back up.

Trembling, I waited for him to talk. His lips pressed down into a hard, gorgeous line of cruelty I wish I could say was more terror than beauty.

"Where," he repeated again slowly, his lips almost moving in a slow-motion cadence. "Did he touch you?"

"Who?"

He grabbed me harder, almost painfully squeezing my soft skin where the rope had burned against my skin. "The man who was in here, where did he fucking touch you?"

"Nowhere!" I yelled, a hot tear sliding down my cheek and colliding with my wrists, with his hands joining us together in my pain, his horror. "H-he came in and said something about me being his. I was kind of out of it, then he left—he left!"

"Motherfucker!" My captor jerked back, and his eyes dripped with hatred as he paced the room. Back and forth, he walked across the wood floor until he finally stopped and looked over his shoulder. "I'll untie you."

"What? Why?"

His nostrils flared. "You'll know soon enough."

Already I could see the erection in his slacks. The way he tried to adjust himself, move out of the light. He left for maybe a minute and returned with a knife. Slowly he cut through the ropes on my ankles and wrists, his whiskey breath on my face.

"Stand."

"Wha—"

"NOW!" he growled from deep within his chest.

I shuffled to my feet. My body was so unbelievably sore. There I stood, naked in front of him. In one swift, rough motion, he clutched onto the back of my neck and forcefully threw my ass onto the bench of the piano.

I barely had time to register what was going on when he sneered, "Play."

"Play wha—"

"Play," he emphasized each letter.

I felt like this was a test that I was going to fail miserably at.

"Juliet," he warned right next to my ear. "If you don't start playing, I'm going to whip your fuc—"

My fingers began moving, and I played what came naturally to me. It was one of my favorite pieces to perform.

There was so much emotion.

So much depth.

Intensity.

Craze.

I played what I was feeling, all the hysteria he was putting me through with his multiple personalities.

One finger right behind the next, my hands danced from one end of the piano to the other. My body and head moving in sync with each other. I got lost in the music, in the vibrations, in the mania of the tips of my fingers, becoming one with the sounds I was evoking. Closing my eyes, I let myself be one with the melody and the life this song was breathing into me.

His vicious words.

His cruel demeanor.

This power he held over me from the moment I'd first seen him.

It was all overwhelming, consuming, breaking me into a million pieces.

Like a shattered doll.

A broken toy.

I. Was. His.

No mind of my own.

No thoughts for myself.

No opinion.

No talking back.

He was stripping everything away from me.

I wanted it to stop.

Please, God … make it stop.

The song was beginning to end, over too soon. I never wanted to let it go. I had to; he would make me. Giving me pleasure and pain was what he did best. I held on for as long as I could, seeking refuge in the only place I always could.

I didn't want to open my eyes. When I did, this would be over—the high I was riding on would come to a complete stop.

I wouldn't be Juliet…

I would only be his pet.

CHAPTER ELEVEN

Donovan

I was sitting in the closet, all the way in the back corner, where he couldn't see me at first. It didn't matter how far back I hid in the darkness; he always found me.

I cried; I couldn't help it.

I didn't like it in here.

"Sir … please let me out. Please, Dad. I'll be a good boy. I promise; I'll be the best boy."

He didn't listen. He never did.

My body was shaking.

I was scared.

What would he do to me this time?

Tears streamed down my face; faster and faster, they fell down my cheeks as I waited for the punishment that always came.

"Shhh … baby … shhh…"

I recognized her soothing voice, knowing who was in my room with me.

"Play for me, Mama," I murmured so low she wouldn't hear what I said.

He didn't like that. When I begged for her. It'd only make him meaner, madder, hurt me more than throwing me in my closet with the door locked on the other side so I couldn't get out.

I was trapped.

Alone.

It wasn't long before I heard her playing on my piano for me. She always did when she could get away from him, long enough to comfort my fear of him. He was never nice. He didn't smile, or laugh, or play with me like I'd see in movies and television shows.

Nothing.

He yelled, and hit, and threw me in the closet. Sometimes it felt like I lived in here, with my sadness and my tears that never stopped. Mama started playing Clair de Lune, my favorite song.

I don't know how many times she repeated it until all of a sudden, I heard his hateful roar, "Did you think I wouldn't have found out?"

She stopped playing, her finger sitting on a key for a second too long.

I gasped, thinking he was talking to me, but he wasn't. I could see through one of the holes in the door that he made one night with a knife. He stabbed it so many times, screaming that I was a bad boy who never listened to him.

I did.

I tried to.

It wasn't enough.

It never was.

"I asked you a question, pet. Don't make me ask you again."

I jumped, hating every second of what was happening, and I couldn't do anything about it.

I was stuck.

I couldn't move, trying to breathe through the terror I was feeling. Exactly how Mama taught me to.

"Master, I don't know what you mean."

"You fucking liar!"

The sound of his whip was the next thing I heard, instantly hitting Mama's skin. I didn't make a sound. Even though I wanted to scream, shout, beg him to stop beating her. Usually, he'd strike her a few times and then stop; this time, he wasn't stopping himself.

"Master, please…"

"Donovan, do you see?! Do you hear your lying whore of a mother?!"

Slap.

Slap.

Slap.

He struck her so many times I lost count. She fell to the floor by the bench of the piano.

Surrendering in mercy.

Usually he would stop. This time he didn't hold back on his assault.

"Donovan…" he sang in that voice I hated more than anything. "Tell him the truth, pet. Where did my boy come from?"

"Master, please… I'm sorry! I'm so sorry!"

"You're a horrible fucking mother, lying to him for this long. I can't trust you with anything, you stupid bitch!"

Over and over, he hit her.

I looked right at the whip with wide eyes, terrified of if he would stop.

Would he?

It didn't feel like it.

"You like that, son?" he asked like he could see me. "Maybe you will turn out to be something and someone after all."

He was in front of the closet in four hard steps, and I instinctively shot back into the wall behind me.

There was nowhere I could go, but that didn't stop my mind from thinking I could hide from him. He unlocked the closet and opened the doors.

Was this a trick?

What do I do?

"Come here."

I looked at my mama from across the room; her face was sad and afraid. She always had the same face when he was around. She wasn't the same mom with him in the house.

"I. Said. Come. Here."

I didn't like the sound of his voice as I moved toward him.

"Crawl to me, Donovan."

"Sir—"

"Did I say you could talk?"

I shook my head, getting down on my hands and knees. Slowly, I did what he ordered.

"This cat o' nine tails, son," he said, moving his head toward it, "carries so much power. You have no idea how much control and power you have with this simple weapon. Now, this is your chance to prove to me that you aren't fucking worthless. I want you to take it and hit your mother. Do you understand?"

I halted dead in my tracks.

"Master..."

"SHUT THE FUCK UP!" he seethed, yelling at Mama. "I'm sick of hearing your voice! I'm having a man-to-man conversation with my son, and if you know what's good for you, you will shut the fuck up before I lose my patience with you!"

I shook my head again, but he cocked his head to the side with a vindictive look on his face.

"Are you saying no to me?"

"Sir, I don't want to," I swallowed, trying to hold back the tears. Knowing it would only get me in further trouble with him.

"Grab the fucking cat o' nine tails, Donovan, NOW!"

Trembling, I did as I was told and grabbed the cat o' nine tails by the handle. It was heavy and felt cold. I wanted to place it back into his hand, but he must have sensed my hesitation because he moved closer to me and wrapped my hand around it, the way it's supposed to be held, he said. Stepping behind me, he gripped onto the handle as hard as he could. His powerful grasp was killing my hand under his.

I tried to focus on that pain instead of what my heart was feeling when he kept ordering me to hit my mom.

Louder and louder his voice became.

I hated the feeling and wanted to scream and run, but I knew it would be worse for my mom if I did. I didn't want him to hurt her anymore. I was tired of seeing him hurt her. She never did anything to deserve it. He had no mercy, and he would laugh and only hit us harder. He said we deserved it, and he would call us all sorts of names. Some I understood, others I didn't.

"NOW," he roared so loud I thought he broke my eardrum.

I could still feel the vibrations of his tone as I hysterically begged, "Please,

Sir, I don't want to ... please..." I couldn't control my tears any longer, and they flowed loosely down my face. I could taste them in my mouth, and it was hard for me to see through each one of them.

"How many times do I have to tell you that real men don't fucking cry! You will grow up to be just like me. Just like your father—that I can promise you!"

I didn't want to grow up and be like him. I didn't want to be anything like the man behind me. He was evil. I hated him, and in that moment, at ten years old, I learned the true meaning of the word.

"DO IT! NOW!"

I closed my eyes, praying that it would all go away. I silently prayed to God that he wouldn't make me do this. That he would stop time or that this was just a bad dream. That it wasn't real. But when I turned to face her, and he ordered me to open my eyes and hit her, I learned in that second, in that moment, that there was no God, or if there was, that he didn't listen or care about my mother and me.

If he did ... what followed next would have never happened.

"When you aim a cat o' nine tails at someone, you make damn sure that you make them bleed. Do you understand, Donovan?"

My mama's face would forever haunt my dreams. She didn't look sad or terrified ... nothing of what I imagined she would. Not that I thought about this ever, but sometimes in my dreams, I'd see her in front of me, saying goodbye. The expression on her face was always devastated; she didn't want to leave.

Though here, she looked relieved as if I were setting her free.

Letting her go.

I didn't want her to leave... What would happen to me if she were gone?

"No, Sir!" I screamed, not caring about the repercussions. "Please don't make me do this, please, Sir, please," I mercifully pleaded.

"DO. IT!"

"Please, Master, please don't make him do this... Have mercy... God ... please don't do this..." She came out of the daze she was in seconds before.

But he didn't wait any longer, and the first slap fell across her back. My hand was pinned beneath his, and even though I wasn't the one inflicting the pain, I still felt it in every inch of my body.

He didn't stop.

He never stopped.

He made me hit her until she wasn't moving.

Until she wasn't breathing.

Until all I could see...

Was her bloody and lifeless body.

I was crying, petrified, knowing nothing would be the same after this.

I knew that like I knew his name, Sir.

"I'm sorry, Mama, I'm so sorry," I openly bawled, barely containing my shaking body and voice as I tried to move her.

The next thing I knew, he backhanded me across the face so hard that I flew across the room. I hit the floor with a thud and immediately hurt all over.

My head was throbbing, and the room was spinning.

It was only just the beginning.

I wanted her arms around me.

Her comfort.

Her warmth.

Her love.

He crudely grabbed my chin, making me look into his dark eyes. "Look what you did, Donovan. You finally proved your worth!"

It didn't matter how many times I had this nightmare play out from my memory; I will never forget what he said next.

It was what made me who I am today.

In my harsh reality, he made me look into his devious glare.

"You're going to be just like me, and one day, you're going to thank me for it."

"NOOOO!" I screamed, gasping for air, sitting straight up in bed.

I was sweating profusely, my mind disoriented, and my bed soaked beneath me. I couldn't tell the difference between my dream and reality. I was shaking all over, and I couldn't catch my breath.

"Are you okay?"

My gaze locked with Juliet's. I must have passed out in her bed with her in my arms.

"What happened?" she whispered, her lips trembling. Reminding me of my mother. "What happened to you? Who is Sir?"

My eyes widened. "My, my, pet. What big ears you have."

"You were screaming."

I was right back in that room with him. It didn't matter that Juliet was in front of me; all I could see.

Hear.

Feel.

Was him.

"Please tell me your name?"

There was something about the way she requested that broke me out of the trancelike state, but I couldn't confess my sins.

At least not right now.

Juliet

I could see the shift in his stare.

I was playing with fire, and that didn't for one second stop me from wanting to know the truth about him. Especially his name.

"Please don't make me do this, please, Sir, please."

His terrified tone reminded me so much of my own.

"I'm sorry, Mama, I'm so sorry."

My head swirled with aftershocks of what I overhead and the way he was looking at me. It held so much sincerity and humanity as if he was another man who was suddenly caring.

"Please tell me your name," I requested again.

But it was over before it even began.

He crudely grabbed the back of my neck, pushing me down onto the floor on my knees in front of him. His fingers raked through my scalp before he grabbed a handful of hair and pulled my head back. I watched him unzip his pants and release his hard, thick cock.

"Look at me. Let me see your eyes."

I did as I was told, peering into the eyes of the man that reminded me of everything that had gone wrong in my life.

This was the first time I'd seen his dick, and it was quite a sight. Still gripping onto my hair, in one quick movement, he thrust his cock right into my mouth with no warning. I gagged at the sensation, his head hitting the back of my throat. Sliding back out and all the way in, he repeated this a couple more times.

I wanted to bite down, and of course, he read my mind.

"Try it and watch how fast I make you bleed for me." Holding me tighter, he ordered, "Push out your tongue. I want my cock all the way in; don't fight me."

I expected him to thrust back in. I was confused when he plugged my nose with his fingers instead.

"You breathe when I fucking let you."

Once again, he shoved his cock to the back of my throat, not letting go of my nose. My head hit the mattress, and I couldn't move. He didn't stop until my lips met his groin, and he held me there for several long seconds.

"Look at me. How am I supposed to know when to let you breathe if I can't see your eyes?"

He pulled out, and I gasped for air while an uncontrollable amount of drool and tears slid down the side of my mouth. Growling and grunting the entire time he fucked my face.

He loosened his hold and let go of my nose, sliding out his dick.

"Breathe."

I did.

Thrusting back in, he used my mouth in the way he deemed fit. I'd never given a blow job before, and I knew this wouldn't be the last time he'd take a first from me.

Should I be grateful he started off with this?

He continued this process until he couldn't take it anymore and came with such force that my entire body shook from his spasms. His hold tightened, making it almost impossible to catch my breath, with an intensity I had never experienced.

Crouching down to my level, he demanded, "Swallow." When I did, he praised, "You're such a good girl."

I smiled, seeking out his attention. Almost falling on my ass as soon as he added…

"I'm always your master, but my name is Donovan."

CHAPTER TWELVE

I had no sense of time. I didn't even know how long he'd left me in that room alone. It could have been a few hours or a few days; everything was beginning to blend together. I wasn't tied to the bed anymore, and I had the liberty to move around. My bones hurt, and my jaw was tender.

Every time I thought about why it was sore, my body tingled in a way it hadn't before. I started to think about what it would be like to have him inside of me. I wasn't an idiot. I knew this was a classic case of Stockholm Syndrome, textbook shit. My picture should be in the dictionary, next to the definition.

Of course, this was what he craved. He was a sick sociopath that I couldn't stop thinking about. Something happened the last time we were together. I didn't know if it was his dream that I witnessed, or him using my mouth as comfort, or maybe it was the fact that he finally told me his name.

All I knew was that I missed him terribly.

Thought about his handsome, devious face.

Dreamt of his hands, his tongue, his cock on me, in me.

What sick twisted game I was playing without knowing the rules or guidelines. It was becoming a slippery slope, my need for his presence, his attention, his body on top of mine.

My mind couldn't decide what state it wanted to be in other than confused and tormented. I honestly didn't know where it came from, all the emotions and feelings. Like a prey, I was caught in his spider web of lies and deceit, and the sad part was I wanted to believe I could change him. All the times he touched me and told me I was his.

It felt real.

Sincere.

Consuming.

I thought about him when I was alone and even when I was lying in his arms. It didn't matter that I knew it was wrong.

Seedy.

Ugly.

And destructive.

I fantasized about all the things he could do to me.

Trying to take my thoughts and desires away from Donovan, Master... I grabbed the silk nightgown on the dresser and put it on. Next, I decided I should use the vanity that was in the corner of the room. Slowly, I made my way over to the seat and sat. Looking at myself in the mirror, I still didn't recognize the woman staring back at me. Grabbing the brush, I began brushing my new shoulder-length blonde hair for the first time. Something about the repetition had me finally relaxed enough to take what felt like my first deep breath since being kidnapped by Donovan's men.

Moments later, I heard the door unlock, followed by his footsteps. I'd recognize them anywhere; I didn't have to turn to know who it was. I stopped brushing, imagining a world where he took the brush and ran it down my hair, holding me tight, telling me that he never wanted to let me go and that he was sorry.

I could be with a man like that.

A man who was strong but who knew my limitations and didn't push them for his sick pleasure. And yet, I still liked the man standing behind me. As much as I wanted to cling to disgust, it was there, that feeling in my chest. Like denying your heart needed to beat was denying he had an effect on me.

"Donovan," I murmured under my breath, loving the way it fell off my lips. Wanting so badly to have his hands on me again.

I waited for his next command, trying to internalize everything I was feeling, but I knew he could smell it on me, feel it in the thick air between us. It was evident he knew me better than I knew myself. My eyes met his when the door shut behind him. His stare went from calm to the treacherous storm that lived inside of him.

"Pet, where did you get that?" he questioned in an eerie tone.

I looked around the room, perplexed by what he was talking about. I didn't know how to answer, and the last thing I wanted was to get it wrong again.

"When I ask you a question, I expect an answer. Why must you always test my patience, Juliet? It's almost as if you want to provoke me."

"I-I-I-I..."

"You-you-you ... what?" he mocked, walking toward me.

I couldn't take it anymore as my body and mind continued to betray me.

"I don't know what you mean!" I found myself shouting, biting the inside of my cheek, and trying to suppress the emotions that were taking control of my being. I bit my cheek so hard I tasted blood, getting it on my lips.

"Is that any way to talk to your master? Where is your respect? Who am I, Juliet? Don't make me ask you twice," he growled it out in a way that was so terrifying I started to shake. I almost preferred the yelling.

I hesitated for a second. "Master..."

He grinned, folding his arms over his chest. "Who am I, pet?"

I swallowed hard. More games, more uncertainty.

"No ... not Master. Who am I? I know you want to say it. Here's your chance ... call me by my name, just like you've been dying to."

I whimpered. "I don't want to play these games. Just do what you want to me."

My stomach churned, and I could practically taste the bile at the back of my throat.

He was standing in front of me when he gripped onto the silk fabric by my chest, and in one fluid motion, he tore it in half—all the way down my body until the gown pooled by my feet. The solitary comfort I had was now stripped away from me. Once he was done, there was no movement or sound for several minutes, and I wondered if he was admiring my body or thinking of all the ways to invoke pain.

Leaning forward, he licked from one corner of my lip to the other. My blood was on his tongue, and our eyes never wavered as he slid it into his mouth and swallowed without any hesitation.

"Get up."

I moved slowly, not wanting to upset him, and the second I stood, he threw the hairbrush across the room, and I was dropped to the ground. With my ass in the air and my forehead resting on the wooden floor, he snatched my arms and held them at my back.

"How many times do I have to tell you that this is how you address me when I walk into the room. Head down, ass up, arms locked behind you. You stay just like this until I tell you otherwise. Understood?"

I nodded, bracing myself for what was to come.

"Now, where did you get the nightgown and hairbrush, Juliet?"

"It was in the room when I woke up."

"That motherfucker."

"What—"

"What's my name, pet?"

"I told you already. It's Master."

"If you don't give me the answer that I want, I'm going to turn your sweet little ass bright red."

"Mas—"

Slap.

"This is what you want, isn't it, Juliet?"

"No!"

Slap.

"No?"

Slap.

Slap.

Slap.

"I don't like being lied to."

"I'm not lying!"

"Bullshit!"

Slap.

Slap.

Slap.

"Call me by my name!"

I couldn't take it anymore, screaming, "Donovan!"

No one could have prepared me for what happened next. It was like I had an out-of-body experience. I watched myself from above, falling to this deep, submissive slumber I didn't think was possible.

I was exhausted from trying to be what he wanted.

Play his doll whenever he demanded it.

The realization was a rude awakening in my alternative state. I went from being scared to euphoric. It made my vision blur, and my eyes shut tight. I couldn't get my legs to move. It was like I was permanently glued to that submissive position on the floor in front of him.

My emotions were all over the place.

My brain was hyperaware of everything.

My body felt strong yet weak.

I thought he carried me over to the bed and laid me in his arms until I saw nothing but darkness again.

Although, I swear…

I heard him talk to me.

Then say my name as he ran his fingers through my brushed hair, sharing, "You'll never be her…"

Donovan

While she slept in my arms, I thought about my life.

"Nothing is the way it's supposed to be, Juliet."

She didn't stir, she didn't awake, so I kept going.

"I wish things could have been different. For you. For me. For us."

I sat there, thinking about all the things I couldn't change. Even if I wanted to, even if I tried— it wouldn't matter. I would still be this man who was a monster.

A villain.

Her captor.

Exactly what that horrible bastard of a father made me. It was like he knew even then how to groom me into an exact replica so that when I looked at myself in the mirror, I didn't see me anymore. I only saw him and my mother's bloodied body.

I felt myself crawling on my hands and knees and then craving the need to default to what he deemed comfortable, normal. And now I was trapped, in a prison of my own making.

In a gilded cage.

A castle nobody was allowed to visit, with all the pretty things placed upon the shelves and at my service, but nobody to share them with, nobody to truly talk to because vulnerability only brought you death.

I knew that now.

Maybe I knew that then?

"I wasn't always like this, you know? You wouldn't leave my mind. I had to know who you are, were, what I could do to you because of what you did to me... It wasn't your fault. But we always pay for our parents' mistakes, right? Isn't that the way it goes?"

My hands shook as I thought back on her brushing her hair with that specific brush, and I couldn't exorcise the vision of my mother sitting on the bed and watching her soothing movements as she brushed her hair and told me in her own way that everything would one day be all right.

It was the hope that landed the final blow.

Not my father.

This unbearable weight was on my chest from the lies, secrets, and betrayal. The tightening in my throat and chest made it almost impossible to breathe; I was asphyxiating in it. I couldn't tell the lies from the truth anymore. I groaned in pain, leaning against the headboard of her bed.

I could let her go and let this be the end of it all. She was mine. I owned her.

My possession to have and hold.

There was no going back for me, only a standstill.

Love, hurt, pain.

Hate.

It was all a tangled web.

I didn't know the difference any more than Juliet did. I wouldn't let her get the best of me, change who I was born to be. I had to continue on, with or without her consent.

This was only the beginning.

The ending was near...

There was so much I wanted to say, needed to tell her; however, I couldn't form the words to explain to her why I was this villain. I had to get away from her. I was spending too much time in this room, with her in my arms. She shouldn't be sleeping on my chest, in my presence. This wasn't part of the process of making her my slave. It was the exact opposite. I was breaking all my own rules, and I couldn't help it for the life of me.

I craved her in a way I'd never yearned for anyone. Especially a woman, a pet, a slave. Although, there was no holding back on hearing her scream my name.

"Donovan!"

I wanted to break her, only to piece her together again. She was an object that I wouldn't lose. I'd have her at my mercy, in my bed, with blood on my hands. I watched her for as long as I could remember, since that first concert I'd seen her when she was eighteen years old, and I was twenty-four. I waited on bated breath for her to be in my embrace. As much as I thought she was just going to be another pet, another beautiful thing I had in my possession, in the back of my mind, I always knew the truth. She belonged to me, and I belonged to her.

Mine.

Always and forever.

Mine.

There was something about her and not just what I knew, saw, and wanted. She had always been different, making a hard man like me go weak. I wasn't supposed to fall for her, it wasn't part of my plan, but I couldn't stop myself.

I needed her.

Longed for her before she was ever in my arms.

There was no going back for me, only going forward with her by my side. Kissing her forehead, I let her go. Leaving her alone in her room, I remembered what it felt like to always be alone after my mother was killed. It was what he wanted, me weak and at his brutal mercy.

He'd taught me everything I know, making me hate who I'd turned into. There was no stopping what I'd become. I embraced it a long time ago. From the moment my father let me out of that closet, I was his to do what he pleased like I was with Juliet.

It was survival.

With a shaky hand, I grabbed my cell phone out of the pocket of my slacks and leaned against the door to her bedroom. Needing the support to hold me up for what I was about to do.

To say.

The phone rang only once when he answered.

I didn't allow Troy to respond.

Simply stating, "She's ready. Let the auction begin tonight."

Fully aware I was only doing this to prove to myself that I didn't love her, knowing in my dark heart that I was born loving her.

CHAPTER THIRTEEN

Juliet

"It's time."

A feminine voice brought me out of my restless sleep. She was wearing a gorgeous white tuxedo set and had diamond-studded glasses perched on the edge of her nose. She looked anywhere between fifty and sixty with her dark hair tucked back into a tight bun, her red lipstick spread across full lips that I couldn't tell if they were natural or not.

Her hands were on her hips as she assessed me. "Well? Aren't you going to get up?"

"Who are you?" I asked in a sleep-filled voice.

Her eyes narrowed. "I'm your fairy godmother."

"What?"

"What, no laughter?" She sighed like she was disappointed. "Guess you really are ready if I'm no longer funny." She turned and said, "I brought two gowns for you to pick from. He's clearly an indulgent master if he's allowing you the choice and not demanding which one to pick. Oh well, maybe it's a test. Choose wisely before I do your makeup and hair, all right?"

She pointed to two floor-length ball gowns. One was a sleek white silk with a fully open back and front. The only lick of fabric on the top would barely cover my breasts and was attached to the slinky skirt. Other than that, I'd need to be careful when I even walked in it.

The other was gold.

For some reason, it spoke to me more. It was simpler, nearly see-through on top except for a few strategically placed sewed-in pieces of golden lace on the strapless top. The rest of the skirt was identical to the white dress, slinky, long, and with a high slit on each side.

"Is there a dinner or something?" I asked, trying to figure out where he'd take me and who would be looking at me.

She snorted out a laugh. "Leave it to Donovan to not even prepare you for your debut, right?" Her tall silver heels clicked against the floor. "Let's just say you're going to a party. There, that sounds better."

I quickly pointed to the gold dress. "I like this one."

"Then let's get it on you," she exclaimed cheerfully as she grabbed the dress from the hanger and slowly unzipped the back. I was already naked, so there was no stripping out of anything as I gently stepped inside the dress, holding it to my chest as she zipped it up.

"Perfect fit. Shocker." She sighed more to herself than to me as she gently pushed me toward the bathroom, where she had a special light you'd use for Instagram photos set up along with a bounty of makeup and hair products.

I could almost believe I was getting ready for a special event.

While she did my makeup and hair, her hands were gentle as she worked, whistling a tune I didn't recognize half the time. I let myself believe I was Julia Roberts and he was Richard Gere.

He was going to wine and dine me.

I'd still be his pet.

But now, we'd somehow be equals.

I'd passed all his tests.

Maybe this was my reward?

"Elaina," Donovan said her name softly, softer than he'd ever said mine, softer than he'd ever spoken to me.

Jealousy at his treatment of her coursed through me as he walked into the room looking like The Phantom of the Opera come to fucking life.

He had an all-black suit on, no color was present, his black silk tie was pinned with a diamond, and he wore a simple black half-mask on his face.

I'd never seen anyone look so handsome in all my life.

And I'd never hated him more.

More than when he shamed me.

More than when he hurt me.

More than when he made me bleed.

I hated him the most when he said her name.

His dark eyes landed on me, and a small smile curved across his full hateful lips as he put his hands gently on Elaina's shoulders and squeezed.

"As always, you did beautifully. How would I survive without you?"

Lowering his head, eyes still on me while Elaina shot me a wink, he kissed her neck, his mouth lingering near her skin.

She froze like she was caught in his web.

He was the spider.

She was the fly.

I was the witness.

Tears of anger burned in my eyes.

Elaina cleared her throat and stepped forward, then turned to face him. "I'll see you tonight, Donovan."

Bile rose in my throat, imagining every possible scenario that would eventually break my spirit, my heart, my soul.

I was still sitting like a good pet when she left the room. Donovan eyed me up and down, so callous and calculating that I didn't even want to imagine all the ways he would make me pay if I chose the wrong dress or addressed him the wrong way.

"You chose the gold," he addressed in a harsh whisper. "I must have trained you well if that's where your eyes fell to ... considering..." He reached into his pocket and pulled out a large Tiffany's box.

I gaped and gasped. Shaking, I reached for it. "T-thank you, Master."

"Ah, she sees a jewelry box, and now she gets it right."

Was he ... teasing me?

It was almost too much. The emotions welled up inside me and threatened to spill over. Adrenaline surged as I slowly opened the box and quickly frowned. It was solid gold and had his name carved inside it along with the phrase. "Mine to take, mine to break. The Society."

He reached for the necklace and held it up. There was some sort of chain attached to it that dangled nearly to the floor and, at the end of it, some sort of handle.

"Turn," he whispered.

I stood and turned around, confused and honored he'd give me something, so... Wait a second... As he clasped it around my throat, everything made sense with stunning clarity.

I was his pet.

Oh God.

I was his pet. I couldn't cry, or he'd punish me and make me bleed. But I was his pet, and this was my collar, and that was his leash. I shattered in that moment, I wasn't sure if it was the last remaining piece of my heart that hoped for something better, maybe even to be rescued by the very man who punished me, but it left.

And I realized he didn't have to beat me into submission. No, he would lead me there with his own hands.

Donovan

I lived for her jealousy, for the way she stared at Elaina like she was going to murder her for gaining my approval.

It meant one thing.

She. Was. Ready.

The limo ride was painfully tense as Juliet gently touched the collar on her neck. *I wondered if she was horrified or excited?* Which would she be, and while I wanted to ask her, I already assumed the answer.

She was, of course, both.

Which made her even angrier.

Juliet liked this role of submissiveness, exactly how I liked the control, the ownership of something so precious, so beautiful, like a rare gem that nobody ever truly deserved but everyone would kill to acquire.

The limo arrived just on time, and I handed her the mask that would match her dress, the one I'd already picked out, and gently attached it to her face. It covered most of it, except her mouth and obviously her eyes, showing every man in attendance that only I could look upon her, however, driving them fucking crazy that they'd never get to see all of her.

Now she was owned.

By me.

A shudder ran through her as the door opened. I was introducing her to the Kingdom I owned, the one I operated, carefully calculated, and inherited from my father. I was showing her behind the curtain, and once she saw it all…

There would truly never be any going back, and I wondered if she knew that, walking into the large ballroom at the estate I'd purchased only for these events. I wondered if she shook with lust, fear, or all of the above. And I hoped, I perversely hoped it was both.

Music swirled around the ballroom, masters danced with their wives while their pets watched and vice versa. The ones being punished were put in a corner. The pets were forced to watch their masters enjoy an evening with their wives, and it killed them to see a smile on their owners' faces while the wives gave them pleasure only the pets could truly give.

There were politicians.

Actors.

Musicians.

There were people of influence and power who no longer knew or understood their own need for dominance until my company offered it to them—for a price.

If I was going to hell, I might as well get rich on my way there.

I gave them life.

And I was in control of it all.

Me and Troy.

Though Troy was starting to worry me, the way he looked at me, the way he saw through even what I refused to understand or process. He'd always been a shrewd businessman, but now he was something else entirely.

Troy was jealous.

And jealousy was a game we never truly played with one another until now.

I watched his face contort into something sinister while I led my pet, her chain wrapped around my wrist as we went to our table, with our expensive wine, our steak, our company for the evening.

"New one." A man whose name I couldn't remember nor would I, added, "She's pretty."

"She is," I agreed. Wrapping the gold chain harder around my fist, I jerked her closer to me and jutted my chin toward the ground by my feet.

She didn't have to be told. Instantly she sat on the floor and bowed her head, waiting for my next command.

I beamed, leaning down toward her ear. "You're such a good girl," I whispered, making her hide back a smile.

"Pity," Troy stated with his pet at his feet. "That you took her before any one of us could even offer."

Pity my ass.

"Yes," I agreed again. "Isn't it, though?"

"Where'd you find her again?" Troy baited me, but I was too smart for him. He was just like my father, always trying to stay one step ahead, and now I knew better.

I would always force him to be one step behind me.

He knew who she was, and pretending he didn't only pissed me off.

"Does it matter?" I shrugged.

Troy laughed, taking a sip of his whiskey. "How about a test, then?"

I wanted to hurt him.

Hard.

Slow.

"You and your tests and theories. What do you need proven? She's mine. I own her, and I can do whatever I want with her."

"Let me borrow her then."

I grit my teeth, and his blue eyes seemed to darken, looking around at the powerful people sitting next to us. Investors, people who could attempt to destroy what I'd built.

"What for?"

"Since when do you deny me one of your pets, Donovan? I thought we shared everything? I mean, unless she's different."

He was testing my patience and my restraint. If I didn't let him have her, he would know how much she truly meant to me, which would only put her in danger when it came to him.

I had no choice but to respond with, "Fine. You don't fuck her, understood?"

"Oh wow, Donovan, so crass. Of course, I just want to see what she can do with her precious hands and maybe, just maybe … how bright her blood is when I make her bleed for me."

Her eyes widened, hearing him announce his last remark.

Anywhere I went, I always had the attention of the room, especially at my events. All eyes landed on Juliet, and the room grew quiet almost immediately, waiting for my next command.

I knew right then and there, this was what Troy wanted. To catch me stumbling when it came to her. He still didn't know who he was fucking with. If he wanted a show, I'd give him an Academy Award performance. You could feel the tension in the ballroom amidst the music, people staring in fascination at Juliet.

With its slits up her thighs, nearly exposing every perfect inch of her.

With her pretty makeup shining for all to see.

Her perfect nails glowing in the candlelight.

Her mask was arranged to hide what I didn't want others to see.

I nearly growled when Troy smiled at her like she was his to smile at. By the time I composed myself, her eyes filled with fuming tears, and I wanted to lean over and lick them as they fell, tell her that in every fantasy I had, it involved those tears of outrage, the blood, the pain.

Let her cry.

Let her bleed.

It only meant more for me to have as her master.

Her chin lifted as I gripped the chain and pulled her closer to my leg. Troy was drawing more attention toward what was mine. He looked around our table, at all the eager faces grinning in excitement for what was to come.

"There's a piano. Let her play, Donovan."

With a confident smile I didn't feel, I tugged on the leash, pulling Juliet's hateful and embarrassed expression toward my face.

"Go play, pet. I'll be right behind you."

I could tell she wanted to yell at me. She wanted to bite, to scratch, to make me bleed the way I'd made her bleed and in front of everyone.

For some reason, it turned me the fuck on, seeing the swirling blues of her eyes, knowing the only object of both her hate and attention was me.

With a smile I knew she'd translate as cruel, I tugged on the leash harder, sending her collapsing at my feet. "But first, a kiss?"

She glowered up at me.

"Kiss my leather shoes," I ordered, playing with her. "And be sure to wipe it off once you're done. You are wearing red lipstick, little one."

I tugged the leash harder when she didn't move, wrapping the chain around my wrist until her head was twisted up toward me.

"Well? What do you say?"

She gritted her teeth and whispered in a hoarse voice, "Yes, Master."

I loosened my hold on the chain, allowing her to lower her trembling lips to my shoe. Chuckles erupted around the table.

"Damn, you trained her fast," a male called out from the guests. "Wish I could break mine in that way."

"She's special," I found myself saying, her lips hovering over my shiny black shoe. Her eyes squeezed shut, pressing against the top.

I felt the hatred dripping from her mouth like a curse. I would never admit how much I loved her mouth on my shoe, but that wasn't the point of my order. I wanted the men in the room to see who she belonged to. It was simply a reminder to Troy and everyone else that she was mine, and I'd fucking kill them without thinking twice about it if they doubted it for one second.

After the kiss, she wiped the shoe with a fingertip, then looked back up at me with swollen lips. Hurt echoed in her eyes, in her posture.

"Thank you, Master."

I nearly dropped the chain. She was thanking me without me telling her. I swallowed a knot of emotion in my throat, jerking back a bit. Realizing I'd just given her power.

"I'll escort her." Troy was suddenly at my side, holding his hand out. He wanted her leash.

Checkmate.

The only thing I could do to prove that she was just my pet, and I didn't care for her.

Was hand it over to him.

CHAPTER FOURTEEN

Donovan

He wanted to play master, dragging her toward the baby grand piano in the middle of the glamorous ballroom, with its hanging chandeliers and dim lighting.

I clutched my hands into fists, took a breath, and reluctantly handed the leash over. "Take care of what's mine, Troy."

"Oh, I always do." He shot her a sinister smile. "Shall we?"

She eyed me for permission; either that or she was petrified. I offered a small nod before he pulled her to her feet, leading her by the small gold chain toward the piano.

Attendants walked up to pull the bench out for her.

Troy looked back at me as he leaned in, whispering something in her ear, and when she nodded at him, he ran a hand from her shoulder down nearly to her ass.

I saw murder.

I wanted to draw his blood and laugh while doing so. I sat and crossed my legs over my knee like this was normal, like I was normal, not internally losing my shit and wondering how soon I could murder my dead father's best friend and business partner.

Troy walked by me and slapped my shoulder the same way he'd caressed hers. Leaning over, he declared, "Think of her playing as a gift that I do hope you enjoy. I know I will."

I didn't tense. "Since when have I ever enjoyed any gift you've given me?"

His eyes turned to steel. "You'll see."

The music started at that moment, and every single shield I thought I had erected came crashing down around me while Juliet started the first part of "I Giorni" by Ludovico Einaudi.

It may as well have been the blanket I held at night when nobody would hold me. It was my safe space. Every single echo of the music took me back to that closet, to a place of so much fear and shame that I wanted to die in front of my guests.

From the second she began playing, I was thrown back to another time, another place, where all I saw was the comfort of my mother—the woman my father had murdered with my hand in broad daylight.

"One day," Mama whispered through the hole in the closet as she sat next to me and put her pinky finger through so she could touch me. I wasn't allowed to hug her.

In terms, that one touch was my oxygen.

It was my strength.

I looked forward to our nightly chats when Father was gone. It meant for one brief second, in a dark room far away from the real world, I was with an angel.

I was with my mom.

She was with me.

And all was right in our messed-up world.

Maybe God didn't exist.

But in that moment, angels did.

"One day," she rasped.

I could hear her tears and wanted nothing more than to take away the pain.

"You will go far away from this place, Donovan. One day, even if I'm not here, I'm going to save you."

"How?" I questioned through blurred tears. "How could you if you aren't here?"

Suddenly her finger was gone, and the start of Ludovico's song played, and I laid against the wall and listened only to have her stop after a few minutes, then come back and whisper, "Did you feel that, Donovan?"

"Yes," I whimpered. "It was really pretty."

"That wasn't music—that, my dear son, was heaven."

"Heaven doesn't exist."

"It exists in music. Music gives us strength. It has the power to end wars, to change emotions, to humanize a person. So wherever you are, no matter what, you feel this music. You listen over and over again, you escape into the heaven I created for you, and you become strong."

"I'm afraid."

She would leave again to play, and for one brief second, I wasn't trapped anymore.

No. I was free.

With her playing her piano for me.

The clapping around me jolted the memory that was wreaking havoc in me. I couldn't stand and didn't want to appear weak. I simply clapped with everyone and watched in utter horror as Troy took Juliet by the leash again and walked her to our table, making an announcement that would set off a chain of events even I couldn't prepare for.

"I'm going to take your little pet to one of the rooms. Her hands play so beautifully, Donovan. I wonder what the rest of her body sounds like." He winked. "That's not a problem, correct? You can even watch. I know you like that."

Juliet's eyes pleaded with mine.

Everyone watched in rapt fascination at our table as if a war was looming, and I'd already lost.

I shrugged like it didn't matter and then gulped down my entire glass of bourbon.

"Let's go."

I thought I knew real shame when my father made me hurt my mom.

91

I was wrong.

Real shame was the look of abandonment in Juliet's eyes.

And sadly, all I could do…

Was look away.

I'd never been more terrified in my entire life, looking around the opulent yet disgusting room. It was a horror movie gone wrong. Donovan was actually allowing me to be in there with Troy.

He'd touch me.

He'd caress me, and my villain was letting him.

Worse off, he would watch it. The man old enough to be my father tugged on my chain, leering at my body.

"You'll enjoy this, pet."

Why did it feel so different when Donovan said it than when Troy said it?

Troy made me feel weak.

Donovan said it, and at times I felt strong, impenetrable. He took me to a different place mentally and physically, and maybe I was crazy, or he was breaking me completely, making me crazy, but for a few short moments in the last couple days, I actually believed he cared.

Oh, how stupid I was…

He clearly didn't. Standing in the corner, arms crossed, face blank—impassive.

I wanted to scream at him.

Beat his chest.

I couldn't.

I wouldn't.

A tear slid down my cheek, and I tried wiping it away when Troy grabbed both of my wrists.

"No, no, leave the tears. It makes it so much more enjoyable to know what you're feeling at all times." While he held my leash, he looked around the room. "Ah, this one, I think."

Still pulling me toward him, he hit a button, the floor opened up, and a giant metal X slowly came up. The floor closed below it with a resounding locking noise.

It truly looked like a typical X made of metal, except there were ropes attached to each end of the letter.

"Troy," Donovan expressed his name like a curse.

He grinned. "I hate it when they squirm too much. A little is enjoyable, but you know how I like things, Donovan. Oh wait, I guess you haven't been in a room with me in quite some time."

"For good reason," Donovan hissed.

"Oh, she'll be fine. Won't you, pet?" He tilted my chin toward him. "Now, be a good little girl and climb onto that X, facedown, arms and legs spread. I need to find something to mar that pretty skin a bit."

Shaking, I shared a look with Donovan only to have Troy grab me by the chin and jerk my head back toward his.

"In this room, I'm your master."

I cried harder, unable to even see the metal X, as I stepped out of my heels and got on the mechanism.

He hadn't tied me up yet, but I knew he would.

Tears continuously slid down my cheeks and onto the ground below me.

How many women had been in here? How many against their will?

I squeezed my eyes shut in preparation and waited for the worst, knowing it wouldn't end here. Silently praying that Donovan would save me.

My villain.

My captor.

Turned hero.

Donovan

She was shaking so hard the table was moving.

I did this to her.

I dangled her in front of the one man with enough money and power to take her. This was on me. He was testing my limits, and if I intervened, he'd know with absolute certainty that she wasn't just my pet—she was so much more than that. Troy circled the X and then stopped in front of a cabinet. He jerked open the doors and made a sound of relief.

"I thought I'd forgotten to put it back after the last time I was in here."

He pulled out the cat o' nine tails and caressed it like it was his child, and suddenly I was back in that room.

Hurting my mother.

My father holding my hands, yelling, forcing, breaking me into a million pieces.

I couldn't breathe.

Couldn't move.

He knew I couldn't bear to look, let alone with him using it on my pet. No, not just my pet. Rage took over as he showed it to her, dangling it in front of me.

"What do you think, Donovan? Nine or twelve hits across this beautiful skin."

His fingertips danced down her spine, gripping her ass in a squeeze that would leave marks later.

He liked marking.

He liked the tears.

The screams, the blood, and the sadistic bastard didn't just do it to get off. He did it because he liked the power. He wasn't a true dominant who cared about their submissive, about their pets, and by the looks of it, he'd only gotten worse.

Juliet continued to shake as Troy reached for the first rope.

"I won't tie you up, but you have to promise not to move. However, you may scream as loud you'd like. Nobody will hear you anyway. Nobody will come. Nobody will care. You're no longer a human. You're property, a pet." He jerked on her leash. "I'm sure you've lied to yourself, imagining someone rescuing you, there is no rescue, and there is no need for it. We set you free, and one day, your heart will simply stop beating because of it." He grinned, lowering his voice. "Now, say thank you, Master, for being so benevolent."

"T-thank." She burst into tears, her body rocking against the table. "F-for…" He lifted the whip and snapped it across her right thigh.

It was a light hit.

But it still pulled back skin, causing her to bleed.

Ordering, "Say it, pet!"

He raised the whip again and struck her much harder, this time on her inner thigh.

She screamed out in pain, loud enough to make me wince. Reminding me of my mother when my father made her take her last breath. There was no time for me to hesitate, no time to realize that my actions would have consequences. I moved on pure instinct.

She wasn't his to hurt.

Mine.

"Juliet, don't you fucking dare!" I seethed, running at Troy and shoving him up against the wall. My fists went flying until his face was nothing but a bloody mess. "You want blood? Now there's your fucking blood!" He stumbled to the floor. I didn't look back. I grabbed Juliet in my arms. "We're going home."

She crumpled into my chest, and I hauled ass out of the room, leaving the piece of shit on the ground in a pool of his own blood.

I walked down that hall with so much anger in my body and no place to release it unless I released it onto her, and with her bleeding and sobbing in my arms, all I could do was walk.

I couldn't speak.

I could barely breathe.

We rounded a corner and nearly ran into Elaina, Troy's wife.

I shook my head. "Clean him up. Room thirteen. I'm sure it's not the first time."

Her eyes filled with worry, nodding. "And not the last."

This was the first I heard of it. "How often?"

Her eyes darted from Juliet's body in my arms to the hallway.

"I'm not at liberty to say."

"Elaina." I clenched my jaw. "Make sure he knows I'm going to fucking destroy him."

Her eyebrow shot up. "Because of a little blood?"

"Because he touched what is mine!"

I shouldn't have even tried talking. I left her there, shaken and confused by my outburst.

Valet had parked my car out front. They usually did when I was in the estate or entertaining.

"Keys," I hissed.

The valet fumbled through the keys and finally found my key fob.

"Thank you as always, Mr—"

"Shut the fuck up."

I opened the passenger door and gently sat Juliet in. She wouldn't meet my eyes as I buckled her seat belt. I ran to my side, hit the gas, and we were off.

But we weren't going to her old room.

No.

She wasn't safe there.

Never again.

Her sniffles filled the car. I drove through the streets of Seattle until I hit the dead end that led to my driveway up on the hill.

While waiting for the gates to open, she must have seen a chance to escape and started pulling at the door.

"Stop," I ordered. "Now."

I tugged her against me. The blood from her thigh was soaking through her dress, and she was shaking, clearly going into shock. I held her there, trying to give her the only comfort I could. The wrought iron gates opened, leading to my mile-long driveway.

A forest surrounded my opulent mansion.

She'd easily get lost and probably pass out from the shock she was in.

Sleeping with the villain was safer.

Wasn't it?

The lights from the main house finally showed as I pulled off the driveway and in front of the garage that housed my car collection.

I parked and went to Juliet's door to help her out.

Her eyes bulged, looking at her surroundings.

Waterfalls surrounded the garage on all sides, flowers, trees; it was my own personal Eden.

It was built for my mom.

She gave me heaven in her music, so I gave her heaven in my home and gardens.

At Juliet's soft gasp, I continued carrying her in my arms. There was no letting her go. This was where she needed to be. I was the only man who could offer what she needed in that instant. She might have been mad at me, and I deserved it. I would make it better. I would heal her if it was the last thing I ever did. I would make it right. I needed to, for her and for me.

I shouldn't have let Troy manipulate me as if I was nothing more than a child, a little boy, the one he had taken under his wing. He'd made me the man I was supposed to be. I couldn't believe how foolish I'd been to fall into his fucking trap.

I knew better.

I was smarter.

Wiser.

Always a step ahead of him.

I let him take her, and the motherfucker even tried to get her to call him Master. He had pushed me to the brink, and I'd allowed it. Despite beating his face in, I still felt weak and at his mercy. He knew now without reasonable doubt what I'd do for Juliet, and that was a power he'd eventually hold over my head.

Fuck.

"The house is mine," I shared, trying to control my reckless emotions and scare her further into oblivion where I couldn't save her. "Over twenty thousand square feet on more than ten acres. Be careful when trying to escape because I know you will. But for tonight..." I nearly stuttered, carrying her through the front door toward the open-aired entry. "For tonight. Stay. For me. With me."

"This is," she finally spoke. "This..."

I carried her toward my bedroom where no other woman, least of all a pet, had ever been.

This was my sanctuary.

My safe place away from the demands of the world I'd created for myself.

I wanted her to see me.

Truly see me for someone other than a villain. I didn't know what had come over me, and I resisted the urge to take her back to her room. It was the order of things, and I was fucking it all up for her and for me.

My feet moved on their own accord, one step after the other until there were no more steps to take, no more feelings to hide, no more uncertainty to bask in.

Just her and me.

Two massive doors opened to my bedroom, and her eyes widened like a deer in headlights when I slowly revealed my paradise.

Setting her on her feet, she waited for my command.

"Good girl," I praised, tucking a piece of hair behind her ear. "Go ahead, I'll allow your questions this time."

She didn't waver. "Why?"

"Why what, pet?"

"Why did you let him take me into that room?"

I growled, pissed with myself. "I shouldn't have, and for that…" Unable to hold back, I willingly gave her what she sought, "I'm sorry."

I couldn't remember the last time I'd said those two words to anybody.

I never apologized. I was never in the wrong. Yet, she needed to hear them, and I obliged her request.

I was sorry.

Wholeheartedly sorry.

She had the power to bring me to my knees, and a huge part of her was starting to see and realize it.

"Do you mean that?" she asked, her gaze filling up with fresh tears.

"I've never meant anything more in all my life, Juliet."

She breathed out a heavy sigh. "I didn't like it. Having him as my master. So please, I beg you, is that what you're training me for? To sell me off to a man like him who will hurt me also?"

I flinched, showing her my true colors before speaking with conviction, "You're mine. I give you my word."

"Your word? Is that supposed to mean something?"

"My word is all I have."

"Then what? You'll share me? Like you did tonight?"

"Tonight was a mistake, and I won't let it happen again."

"What does that mean?"

"It means you're mine. *Only* mine."

Her lips trembled. "And what about you?"

"What about me, pet?"

"Does that mean you're mine too?"

"My, my, Juliet. Remember, pet, curiosity killed the cat."

She smiled, despite herself. "You can't do anything more than what you've already done to me."

"And what's that?"

"Made me yours."

"Not quite, but we're getting there."

"Is this your plan?"

I arched an eyebrow, cocking my head to the side.

She answered my rebuttal without me having to say anything.

"Is your plan to make me crave you and the things you do to me?"

"I haven't done anything you don't want or need."

She scoffed out in disgust, throwing her mask to the floor.

"If you would have said that to me yesterday or the day before, I would have laughed in your face."

"And now?"

"Now, I don't know what to think. You did that to me. Made me question everything. Are you proud of yourself?"

"I take pride in anything that involves you, Juliet."

"I hate you," she spat. "Do you hear me? I. Hate. You."

Grinning, I stepped back and waited.

In less than a second, she dropped to her knees and apologized, "I'm sorry! I'm so sorry, Master! But I do hate you! I do!" she screamed for herself. I already knew the truth.

I let her have her pity party, her temper tantrum, her defiance. It was the least I could do after what I'd put her through tonight. Crouching in front of her, I grabbed her chin to force her to look at me.

"You and I both know there's a very thin line between love and hate, little girl."

She swallowed hard, listening to my every word.

"I want you to hate me, but I also want you to love me."

"Why? I don't understand. Please make me understand."

Nodding to the piano in the corner of my suite, I said, "Play for me, Juliet."

"Ugh!" She jerked her chin away like a child. "Just answer my question! Why do you want me?"

"Why not?"

"Stop it! Stop with your games! I want to know the truth! I deserve to know the truth!"

"You don't make demands, pet. That's not your role to play."

"Play? Exactly! This is just a game to you! I'm just a fucking game! Your play toy, your doll that you share with perverted bastards just like you are!"

My patience snapped, and I heard it loud and clear. Roughly gripping onto her chin again, I sneered, "I'm nothing like them, and don't you ever fucking forget it."

Meaning every last word.

CHAPTER FIFTEEN

Donovan

Yanking her chin out of my grasp, she lost her shit, and again, I allowed her to. I hated having to endure this emotional bullshit, considering I never had before.

I guessed we were both learning new things.

In a high pitch, she shouted, "You shared me! You shared me, Master! How could you do that to me? How could you let him hurt me?"

"How about we get your story straight, Juliet? I beat him within an inch of his life for you. I stopped him, didn't I?"

"You still handed me right over to him, knowing what he wanted to do to me!"

"What bothers you more, pet? The fact that I let him hurt you, or the fact that you wish it was me who was doing so?"

"To hell with you!"

I lunged at her, and instantly she fell to her back with my body hovering above her petite frame. Caging her in my arms on the sides of her face, I leaned down, close to her lips, and spewed, "I'm already there, and I've been there since I was ten years old."

She gasped, and her lips parted. Understanding my subtle yet pungent reply.

"Who is Sir?"

Through an overwhelmingly clenched jaw, I bit, "My father."

She grimaced, not trying to hide it, hurting for me without me having to make her.

"So what happened?"

"If I tell you, what do I get out of it?"

Her steep breaths came out in ragged pants, her chest was rising and falling, and I knew if I touched in between her legs…

She'd be wet.

For me.

"I'll play for you."

"You'll play for me regardless. Try again."

"I'll be a good girl. I promise. Please give me something, Master. Please…"

Looking her up and down, I thought about it for a second. My father didn't try hiding what he'd done. It wasn't the first time a slave would die at her master's hand. Our world wasn't for the weak, and if that meant someone died, then so be it.

Life went on.

"Did your father do something to your mother?"

"You could say that."

"Tell me. What happened? Maybe I can help you."

"Help me?" I jerked back.

"Yes, do you forget who I am?"

"I know who you are, Juliet. It's one of the main reasons you're here with me now."

"What does that mean?"

"It means I owe you no explanations. I owe you nothing."

She actually batted her fucking lashes at me.

"For fuck sake. If you must know, the cat o' nine tails, the same one that Troy used on you tonight. It was my father's, and with his hand gripped over mine, he beat her with it until she took her last breath in front of my eyes."

"Oh, Donovan," she uttered in a breathless tone. My name fell off her lips.

In pity.

In pain.

In the realization that Donovan and Master were two different men. At least when it came down to her, they were.

"When I say I'm untouchable, I mean it."

I tried to see things through her eyes. With a heavy sigh, I hung my head.

"Juliet…"

She caressed the side of my face, touching me of her own free will for another first for us tonight.

"Your father made you this way."

"No, Troy did."

"I don't understand."

I shook my head. This conversation was over. I shouldn't have indulged her, to begin with.

"That's enough questions for tonight."

"But—"

The stern expression on my face was enough to render her speechless. I stood, taking her with me.

"Be a good girl and sit on the edge of the bed for me. Understood?"

She nodded, and I turned to walk into my ensuite bathroom to grab the cold cream and a bandage. When I returned, she was sitting in the spot I told her to. In less than a couple of steps, I was standing in front of her with her eyes staring up at me. Grabbing the hem of her gown, I pulled it off her body and threw it toward the garbage. It was ruined; the mere sight of it would make me angry, but not as angry as I was taking in the wound on her thigh.

"Motherfucker," I rasped, getting down on the balls of my feet to clean her up and tend to her wounds.

She was now naked before me, the way she was meant to be.

Her hand reached the side of my face, and with the back of her fingers, she caressed my cheek. Fresh tears spilled from her eyes.

"Thank you, Master. For apologizing, for taking care of me. For… I don't know… everything."

Unable to respond, I simply nodded instead.

"You swear, you promise that you'll never share me again? With anyone? Even if I'm bad and you're punishing me, it will always be by your hands?"

I kissed her fingers, stating, "I swear to you on my life."

"Okay," she breathed out. "I forgive you."

Three little words I didn't know I desperately wanted her to express until I heard them fall off her lips and into the palm of my hand. After I made her better, I kissed along her freshly cleaned wounds like my mouth would heal her.

"Now, you'll play for me, pet. I need the music. Show me heaven … again."

She grabbed my face, and her lips were over mine before I realized she was kissing me for the first time.

Excruciatingly slow.

Soft.

Tender.

As if she was my angel.

My willpower to stay away from her was fading more as the days went on. I actually looked forward to coming into her room. Wanting to be with her like she was my whole world, to see her smile, to watch her lips move, to listen to her play the piano for me.

But most of all, to have her in my arms.

In my bed.

Every night.

Every morning.

You see, she wasn't the only one falling.

I was hers.

Only hers.

And I'd been so since the first time I'd seen her and knew who she was. I was falling for her. Fuck, I had already fallen for her, which was a deadly combination for a man like me. Because I knew the ending wouldn't be happy. It couldn't be; not between her and me, not at all.

To be in love was the biggest sign of vulnerability. I might as well have put a fucking bullseye on my forehead and hers too. Death always came early when you had something to lose. And Troy? He knew that, lived for it.

I slid my tongue into her mouth, and she moaned in delight.

Feeling me.

Tasting me.

Being one with me.

I pecked her lips one last time before she rasped, "I'll play for you, Donovan, but please … just be you tonight. That's what I need. That's who I want. No Master. No pet. Just Juliet and Donovan."

Bringing my attention to what she was implying. I would disappoint her. I wasn't her hero. I had no idea how to be. How to be the man who would become one I'd forgotten, one I'd destroyed long ago. It didn't matter. My dark heart wanted to try, even though my mind knew it was useless.

Standing up, I held my hand out for her to take. She did, and within moments she was sitting on the piano bench I'd purchased and dedicated to my mother. It wasn't the one she played. That Baby Grand was in Juliet's room. This was a replica of it.

Her fingers began moving, playing the song she was playing earlier in the evening. The one Troy had told her to play in front of all of my guests, fully aware of what it meant to me.

What it did to me.

The pain and pleasure.

The sorrow and happiness.

The heaven and hell.

The only one able to soothe me. I couldn't even think or focus. I just wanted to listen to the music, to the notes as they swept into the universe around me, becoming my air, my Eden, my soul. In one moment, she'd both broken me and then saved me again. Little by little, she was healing the broken man who lived inside of me—the one who wanted every last inch of her.

From her heart.

To her soul.

To her fucking pussy and every hole she had in her body. I wanted ownership of everything that could be and would be mine. I watched with the certainty of what she was doing to me. How she was breaking me down, faster and faster her fingers played the keys, getting lost in the symmetry of what she was evoking.

Once again, my feet moved on their own accord, like I was being yanked by a rope, a chain of nothing but agony and distress. Placing my hands on top of hers, I pressed down on the keys while she played the song perfectly.

She tensed, understanding I could play the piano just as she could. My fingers slowly ran across hers as we played in unison, as we became one in a way we never had before. Sharing the music. Sharing the joy, the pain. Sharing what made us feel, what cut the deepest, and what created the chaos of emotions that surrounded us and made us into monsters or men.

I remembered wanting to play like my mother. Even before my father took her away from me, I always had that thought in the back of my mind, that little voice would make itself known, and subconsciously I would think about what would happen if she was gone.

Where would the music go?

It needed a place to go. And that place had to be me. I made sure she taught me everything she knew, and sometimes I played for her when she needed heaven. I played for her just like she played for me. I needed it. Craved it. Not just for me, but for her.

I stared down at Juliet, lust pounding through every vessel in my body. I stood behind her and touched from her neck to her breasts, to where I wanted to be the most.

Her pussy.

She was wet.

Silky.

Tempting to eat.

I had yet to thrust my tongue into her heat. As if I was a possessed man, I stood in front of her now, and in one swift, sudden movement, I shut the top board of the piano and placed her on it instead. Her feet hit the keys, she gasped at the turn of events.

I slid her down to the edge, yearning to close the distance between us.

"Tell me, Juliet. Tell me what I want to hear. Who do you belong to?"

Her frenzied gaze found my serene one.

I was sedated.

Still.

At peace in this hell I lived in.

With her in my arms, everything just felt right. She opened her mouth, hesitating for a few seconds. As if she knew that once she said it, there was going back, only forward in this game of cat and mouse where I chased and she ran.

"I'm yours."

My heady hands slid down her body, needing to touch her.

Own her.

Fuck her.

"Tell me again."

"I'm yours, Donovan."

My name.

The way she said my name.

I was somehow forgiven.

No longer a sinner.

No, I was a saint.

Worshipped.

Revived.

Holy.

And for the first time in my life—deserving.

Spread wide, she was vulnerable, ready.

"Again," I demanded in a harsher tone than I intended, needing to hear the soothing words like a balm to my soul.

"I'm yours," she repeated while I kissed and licked my way down every last inch of her skin.

"Yes, you're mine, Juliet." Answering her question from earlier, I confessed, "And I've always, always, been yours."

Juliet

My stomach fluttered.

My heart dropped.

With what he had just admitted to me.

Sitting on the bench, his eyes devoured me in a way he hadn't before. Staring directly at the place no man besides him had ever seen. I was nothing, completely at his mercy, and yet I felt powerful as his breath exhaled across my core.

Cocking his head to the side, he narrowed his eyes at me. "By all means, Juliet, spread your legs wider for me."

"I—"

He leaned forward, placing his tight grip on my waist, having my back fall against the top board.

"That wasn't a suggestion. I want to fuck your cunt with my tongue."

I angled up onto my elbows and did as I was told. Slowly, he eyed me up and down with a look I'd never seen before.

"Wider," he roared in a primal tone.

I jumped, overwhelmed. Seeing this side of him emerge was unsettling and arousing. I looked into his vacant eyes, silently pleading for the man he was minutes ago.

He glanced down at my heat before quickly moving his calculated gaze back to my eyes.

"Touch your pretty little pussy. I want to watch you come for me, Juliet."

"Can you—"

"No."

He didn't waver. Dark, tantalizing eyes eagerly waited for the show. Taking a deep, steady breath, I desired to please him. Spreading my legs further, I moved my jittery hand where he ordered me to touch myself, hissing upon contact on my clit. The nub was still sensitive from his assault the day before, where he'd slapped me into submission, throwing me into this euphoric hole.

I arched my back as he watched, waiting for him to tame me, to pick me up if I needed punishing. I wanted to be blacked out to see myself, my face, to know that I was who I believed I was when he told me to do the things I did. I needed that proof, that touch, that feeling washing over me again and again.

He arched a demanding eyebrow, waiting impatiently as always. He was standing right in front of me, watching me with an expression I couldn't read, once again a blank canvas, a mystery, a monster in plain sight. So frustrating!

"That's right, Juliet. Just like that."

His sultry voice set my nerves on fire. It didn't take long for my body to respond, working my clit harder and more demanding than I ever had.

I didn't do this often, but when I did, I fantasized about no one in particular.

This time, I only saw him through my hooded eyes. My legs trembled the closer I got to giving him what he wanted. I couldn't hold back any longer. As much as I wanted to stare into his eyes, my body betrayed me.

My back arched against the piano while my lips moaned his name, "Donovan…" I shattered from the most intense orgasm.

Panting profusely, I tried to catch my bearings from what had just occurred between us. Anxiously waiting for his next move, I felt him before I saw him. His face buried in between my legs. Not giving me a chance to recover from the high he had just inflicted.

His tongue was relentless.

Licking from my opening to my clit.

Working me over with his skilled mouth.

I let him have his way. Every last part of me belonged to him.

I knew that now.

I knew that then.

Maybe he was the reason I existed in the first place. I relaxed at the thought.

I was confused.

Torn.

Conflicted.

This wasn't me. And yet, he made me feel like maybe, just maybe, this had been me all along.

Shaking away the hasty feelings, I moaned, "Ah…" my back arched off the piano again.

He slid his fingers into me while sucking hard on my clit. His body took on a whole different demeanor. The cold, callous bastard was gone, and the lenient and giving man from minutes ago appeared out of thin air like he never left this room.

He was being gentle with me, afraid I would suddenly break in another way than he brutally craved. His mouth and fingers taking their time, making love to me, building me up, and letting me enjoy the sweet torture of his tongue.

My body began to tremble, a feeling only he could generate within me. There was something different about him in that second. He was living in the moment, feasting on me like he needed to prove he owned my body, mind, and soul.

He wanted me to feel worshiped, my body burning for him in every way possible. He fed me what my soul needed. My heart rapidly beat in my chest, making it difficult to breathe. My breath became erratic, urgent, and heady. Falling over the edge repeatedly.

"Oh, God," I screamed out in a voice I didn't recognize, climaxing so fucking hard I saw stars behind my eyes.

I withered around, coming down from the pleasure, feeling loved and adored. I hadn't realized he released the hold he had on my thighs and was hovering above me within seconds. His large muscular frame made me feel so tiny, so safe.

Trust me, the irony was not lost on me.

I knew my monster.

He knew me.

This was no fairy tale.

This was life.

It was hard.

And it was mine.

I couldn't wait to stare into his serene eyes, to feel as though he was owned by someone other than himself. Mine, once again. Savoring the feel of his secure arms and his hard cock against me, I breathed in his masculine, addicting scent.

Feeling his breath along my lips, he praised, "You're such a good girl, Juliet. Such a lovely, beautiful girl. How can I stop myself from wanting to own every last part of you?"

My hooded eyes stared into his lust-filled ones.

Passion.

Self-loathing.

Never imagining I would see the man, hear what he was confessing.

My eyes widened, tranquil and at peace. Immediately wanting this roller coaster of emotions to consume me.

"There's a very thin line between love and hate, little girl."

He was right.

He didn't falter, standing up between my legs, sliding the zipper of his tuxedo pants down. He didn't even get undressed. With a devious grin, I caught the wetness of my orgasm down his mouth and chin. He wore it like it was his prize, like it was his honor, like it was everything he'd ever wanted and needed to become whole.

Roughly, he tugged my thighs toward him, effortlessly sliding my heated body toward his dick. Placing me where he wanted me, I was now a couple of inches away from his hard cock.

I'd never seen another man, but Donovan was stunning.

Big.

Firm.

Wide.

He would break me with it, and I didn't care. I was his to do with what he saw fit. I was a virgin, and he knew that. Sliding his hand up and down the length of his shaft, he jacked off in front of me. It was such an erotic sight to witness, and I couldn't tear my eyes away from what he was doing to himself. He fisted his dick harder and harder, confirming my suspicions.

"I don't make love, Juliet. I can't … I won't."

CHAPTER SIXTEEN

My mouth parted, and I licked my dry lips. Watching the tormented man in front of me, making me want him even more.

He waited for me to say the words, "I don't care. Fuck me then."

Pressing my fingernails hard into my skin, I braced myself for his thrust that would soon come. I'd witnessed both sides of this broken man.

The good and the bad.

His heaven and hell.

Pleasure and pain.

His love…

His hell.

The villain wasn't asleep anymore. No, I'd awakened the sleeping beast, and he'd finally come out to play. He leaned over, his lips getting close to my face, his cock at my opening.

In a sick and twisted way, I wanted this. His dominance had become an aphrodisiac for me. He kissed my lips with so much urgency that I could have come from that alone. When his tongue touched mine, I moaned, and it was in that instant that he thrust inside of me with one hard shove, filling me to the hilt.

I loudly gasped as my body jerked forward from the intrusion through my virtue.

"I take, Juliet. I don't know another way to be, to live. This is the man I am, but for you… I wish I could be different."

His body trembled against mine; his words were kind against his harsh actions. I gripped onto the edge of the piano, biting my lower lip until I tasted blood. This was happening. My happily ever after with my villain, bringing me home but not mine, his, he was pulling me into his home, his world, and I was helpless as I fell for him and all his deviousness.

His tongue licked from one end of my lips to the other. I tasted myself as he swallowed my blood, sliding out and back in.

This was our beginning when it should have been our ending.

A final taste.

A hello mixed with a bloody goodbye.

Thrusting in and out, he didn't let up. My hands instinctively reached for him for comfort, for support, for something, anything. With one grip, he crudely pinned them over my head, not allowing me to touch him, even for one second.

I couldn't feel his warmth, only his turmoil. Suddenly, his demeanor changed, showing me the connection, the love which I longed for more than anything.

"Stay," he ordered in a light murmur, moving his hand from my wrist to touch my clit instead.

I panted, instantly feeling the craze he was stirring. I was still sensitive from his assault with his tongue. Tears rolled down my face, and I couldn't hold back the moan that escaped from my throat.

He growled from deep within his own, toying with my clit as he licked away my tears.

Side-to-side.

Up and down.

He drew out another orgasm, owning even my pleasure in that moment.

I was wet.

Slippery.

My blood on his dick.

His eyes bore into mine, and I half shut my gaze, about to come.

"Don't you dare close your eyes."

I tried to keep them open, and he angled his forehead on top of mine. Fucking me harder, faster, his fingers worked overtime.

I cried.

I begged.

Until he won what he sought.

My come.

I couldn't stop.

Taking me how he really wanted, making me feel like I was his—owned. Thrusting in and out of me with such abandonment, such hunger, fighting a battle of love versus hate. More tears slid down my face as he kissed them all away. Our eyes locked, and he showed me everything I so desperately wanted to see.

A roar erupted from his core, allowing his demons to prevail.

He came deep inside of me.

I came again.

It was such a crazy thing that was happening. One minute I was hurting from his cock, the next, I was coming on it.

Through our entwined bodies, I tried to stay in this moment with him; however, it was no use. My mind was thrown into another rational thought.

We didn't use a condom, and I wasn't on the pill.

Did he know that too? What was he trying to accomplish here?

His body collapsed over mine, shoving my questions away like he did my sanity. I heard him groan and felt him shudder, shaking my body from his own orgasm. This was supposed to be his way of freeing me from his hell, except it was the opposite. He only dragged me along with him, burning me alive with his demons and mine.

I hissed when he pulled out, immediately feeling the loss of him. He kissed my sweaty neck and left me there alone, with so many questions I didn't even know where to begin.

I stayed put.

I didn't move an inch, afraid of what would happen if I did. He wordlessly shuffled around the room and disappeared into the bathroom. I closed my eyes, letting several tears stream down the sides of my face and onto the piano that would forever hold a part of us. Setting my hand over my heart, I waited for him to return.

When he finally did, I tried to breathe and shut my eyes as tight as I could. If my eyes were open, he would know. If I made a sound, he would know he meant something to me even when he shouldn't.

Not strong enough to look up into his eyes, too weak to handle what I would see or what I wouldn't, I continued to painfully squeeze my eyes shut, keeping the tears in place.

I heard his footsteps, walking back toward me. My legs were spread, and I felt a warm washcloth between my legs and down my thighs. He was cleaning me, tender, caring, slowly, from my core to my feet.

He had officially broken me, except this time…

Those broken pieces welded together with his.

We were one.

Jaded.

Fucked up.

In love.

He was the first to break the silence, declaring the truth I already knew, "This is the closest to making love that you're going to get from me." Licking off one last tear, he added, "Best get used to it now."

Donovan

I was a monster.
A villain.
A bad, bad man.

However, for the first time in my life, I wished I could be different. Not for me, for her.

My Juliet.

After I tended to her, I carried her to my bed. She watched as I undressed, getting into bed naked, where she fell asleep in my arms.

This was my sorry excuse of a fucking life, and I was dragging her into the pits of hell with me. She didn't deserve it, and I would never let her go.

Give her back.

Mine.

No matter what.

I contemplated if I was really going to do this, for days, for nights, the entire time she slept in my arms. All I knew was there was no going back from here. She wouldn't return to her room, to the stuff I'd bought for her, to her comfort I'd created out of pure chaos. She would stay in my bed, in my suite, sleep in my arms every night and wake up in them every morning.

I'd keep her with me, always.

Sometime during the night, I must have fallen asleep, which was unusual for me. You see, villains never sleep. They prowled with an evil energy that caused their minds to continue to work overtime, wondering what the next conquest would be when they'd get their next pull. Being a villain was like being hooked on cocaine. You were always waiting for your next hit, wondering about it, dreaming, wishing—except for the first time in a very long time, I wasn't the villain who stayed awake and plotted. I was the one who went to sleep and actually slept.

The comfort she provided without even knowing it was found in her arms, in her warmth, in her tight pussy wrapped around my cock.

I'd never taken a woman's virginity. It was too personal, too private, and I never wanted my slave to think she was mine in that way. With Juliet, the moment I learned she was a virgin, I fucked my fist to the visions of taking her for the first time. Her blood on my dick, her cries of pain, her moans of passion...

They all belonged to me now.

I owned every last part of her, just how I intended before I even had her taken.

My mind was made up as soon as she laid in my bed, wearing nothing but the flesh on her skin. I tossed and turned, shooting straight up from sleep.

I didn't feel her.

I couldn't see her.

Fuck.

"Pet," I announced in an eerie tone, glaring around my empty bedroom.

Realizing very fucking quickly what I had to do, I darted out of bed and threw on my tuxedo slacks as I made my way out of my suite. Taking the fucking stairs two at a time, I didn't want to waste a minute waiting for the elevator.

My feet pounded against the cold steps, echoing through the stairwell and down each corridor. A fucking rope tugging me to her, I reassured myself repeatedly that she was still there with me.

Safe.

"Juliet!" I shouted at the end of the stairs.

No answer.

Not one.

Fuck.

I ran from one room to another, shouting her name from the rooftops. Panic began settling in, and I swallowed it back down.

Did she escape? How?

My estate was crawling with guards, so she couldn't have gone far. Slamming the door open to the kitchen, I walked in on Juliet sitting on the island naked, eating fucking cereal.

"Hey, were you calling my name?"

"You could say that."

"Oh." She smiled. "I was hungry, and I didn't want to wake you."

I stepped further into the kitchen, enjoying the naked Juliet show for a minute. My cock strained against my slacks from the sight of her perfect pink pussy, still glistening from the night's events. Her soft moans filled the room, making me think twice about the fact that I wanted to put her over my knee and tell her she was a very bad girl for leaving my bed without permission.

My dark impulses seethed at me to make it right, show her that she was supposed to be obedient, and I was her master.

Deep down, I knew she felt and saw each and every moment of weakness, including now. That was how profound our connection was, which was all the more reason I needed to set the plan back into action.

I couldn't.

I wouldn't.

Even if I wanted to, I didn't.

I would die before I ever let anything happen to her. Thinking about my life, I came to terms with the fact that Juliet was the first woman I ever truly, wholeheartedly was falling for.

She was made for me.

And maybe, just maybe, I was made for her too.

That realization alone nearly brought me to my knees.

I didn't think twice about it as I stepped in front of her. Not giving a flying fuck what was right or wrong anymore, or what I had to do, I grabbed her bowl of cereal. Resisting the urge to laugh at the sight of her, with wide eyes, she peered at me. Ready to get down on her knees and beg for forgiveness if she needed to.

Whatever it took to please me, that much was clear and evident on her beautiful face.

In one fluid motion, I pulled her into my arms. Holding her close against my chest for a second, she froze, not expecting my abrupt gesture.

Despite wanting to punish her, I wanted her comfort more. Before I knew what I was saying, I breathed out, "You're such a good girl for not trying to escape."

She relaxed instantly in my arms before pulling away to hold my face in between her hands. I'd never allowed anyone to touch me, and more than that, to comfort me.

"Did you think I would leave you? Even after what happened between us tonight?"

I hid back a smile. "What happened tonight, pet?"

She blushed... her cheeks a rosy red. Reminding me of her luscious ass when I spanked her into submission. Memories from our encounters came flooding back, trying to find the calm to my storm. I wanted to tug that hair with my fist and pull her down across the floor just so I could look at her, just so I could see that wide-eyed lustful expression and know it was all for me.

With a stern and sincere expression on her face, she replied, "You made me yours."

My chest tightened. This feeling. *What was this feeling?* My lips parted as I whispered back to her, "Pet, you've always been mine."

"And tonight, you proved it," she said immediately.

"To you?"

A slow nod.

"I see."

"Do you?"

I arched an eyebrow, still holding her in my arms.

"Do you see me, Master? Do you see what you've done to me?"

I froze, unable to hide in the shadows anymore without her knowing. I couldn't take my eyes off of her, mesmerized by her beauty, her nature, her fucking heart. The way she poured her heart and soul out to me like it was one of the easiest things to do. I'd never seen her look so breathtakingly stunning before.

She was glowing.

Radiant.

Dripping with sexuality and this confidence that was so addicting I wanted to taste it.

As if she had newborn skin, a new identity, for a moment, I didn't recognize the woman staring back at me. Like we were the only two people in the world. She was so full of life, so happy in her element, so content in her surroundings. The dark cloud I shadowed over her had been lifted, breaking free from the hold I was suffocating her in.

Did I do this? Did she? Or was it just the perfection of us together?

I leaned against the island, needing the support. I hung my head, my heart and mind raging war with each other. Wanting to take her back to my room and have my way with her, cherish her, show her how fucking crazy she made me.

I looked into her mesmerizing gaze, memorizing every last thing about her in this moment between us.

Everything I loved.

Everything I cared about.

Everything I needed…

Was right there in front of me.

In my embrace.

In my distress.

My home.
My hell.
She was heaven.
An angel.
For another first tonight.
For the first time in my life, I stared into her hopeful eyes…

And started to believe there was a God, and he'd sent her here for me.

CHAPTER SEVENTEEN

Juliet

One month later

During the day, I was his slave.

But during the night—he was mine.

His moods changed as swiftly as the Seattle weather, just like shared smiles, touches, and punishments.

I never knew which side I was going to get from him. There were a few things that had changed since that first night on the piano, and one was his insatiable hunger.

I never went to bed clothed—neither did he, for that matter—and every evening felt like some religious experience where his hands gripped me only to follow with a caress like he'd forgotten he was touching something that could break.

My days were long, filled with useless and demeaning tasks he needed me to finish, like making sure I was constantly clean for him, ready for his mouth, ready for his touch. But you could only shower so many times, and I was getting more and more bored by the minute.

Besides, you couldn't just have sex twenty-four-seven, and he was gone all day, leaving me to lounge around the house. Yes, he let me roam now. Not that I could escape anywhere with the number of guards he had on his estate. I swear, I turned, and there was another man who I hadn't seen yet. I thought my father was paranoid, but this man took the cake. I often wondered if it was like this before me or it was only like this now because I was held captive by him.

Though, was I?

I had food.

I had a pool.

Several places to walk.

TV.

I had freedom in his home, which only further confused my role in his life. *How much more liberty would he allow?*

I wasn't used to being idle, and despite having free range of his entire property, including the rose garden outside, and the miles and miles of land that he owned, I was still unfulfilled. When I finally discovered the home gym, I nearly burst into tears only to have him punish me later and whisper in my ear, "Lose that ass, and I'm marking it."

He'd pinched my skin so hard I was afraid it was going to bruise. After that, I did a lot of air squats and constantly walked around sore, almost like a reminder of his threat and my new promise.

Keep the ass.

There were cameras everywhere in his home, and it didn't surprise me that he was watching my every move.

Would it always be like this, or would he eventually trust me? Did I trust myself? Did I want to leave?

No, I didn't. And that was the hardest pill for me to swallow.

The sound of the door slamming shut had my heart racing as I made dinner in his elaborate kitchen. I'd never made him food before.

I wasn't even sure I was allowed to.

But I was again so bored it was worth the punishment for whatever he thought was appropriate at my taking control and the lead.

Even after all those punishments, after all that pain, and trust me—he still invoked a lot of pain. There was always pleasure that followed. Naked, pounding into me, pulling my hair, and screaming my name like it was his religion.

Everything happened at night, and it was when he was truly mine. There was something about the darkness that permitted him to let his guard down with me. Not sure how much more capable he was at letting me in, but it didn't stop my mind from hoping that I'd eventually own him entirely.

"What's this?" Donovan pulled off his suit jacket and threw it over one of the barstools with his steely eyes focused in on the lasagna that I'd attempted to make for him. "Pet..." He frowned. "You have many jobs, but none of them include cooking."

"Sorry, Master." I gritted my teeth. "I just wanted to do something since I can only watch so much TV and shave the hair off my body..." I didn't mean to add that little bit in at the end because he always wanted me bare, but really, how much could one person tolerate as far as boredom?

He froze, and then in a harsh whisper, "Are you saying you aren't happy with your master, pet?"

"No!" I blurted. "That's not it; I just..." I frowned again and gripped the countertop, embarrassed that my stupid lasagna looked so bad, and it would be a point of contention. I couldn't do anything and was only using his body while he used mine.

I wanted more.

But I was terrified of speaking it out loud, and maybe I was sick in the head, but the idea of leaving him, of leaving this, had me panicking all over again like I was trapped back in that room by myself instead of next to him, in his arms.

Donovan pulled out a chair, the sound nearly deafening as he dragged it across the kitchen floor. He crossed his arms and stared.

"Do I not fulfill all your needs?"

"You do, Master. You do," I lied.

His lips curled into an amused smile. "You need to work on that, your ability to make me believe things..." He sighed. "Open a bottle of wine, two glasses, and let's discuss..."

I froze and then did exactly that, grabbing the first bottle of red from the cellar I could find along with two glasses.

When both were poured, I stood next to him, unsure of what to do. *Was I allowed to sit? In a chair? His lap? The floor?*

Most of the time, he fed me from his hands.

"Sit," he demanded.

Still, I paused, my hands twisting in front of me as they clung to each other, afraid I would reach for him by accident, afraid I'd never let go.

And that was the issue.

I wanted him.

I never wanted to let go.

But he was the same person as before.

Unable to realize that some of the things we wanted the most, we could never have, even if they were right in front of us, begging to be seen.

Slowly, he pulled out a chair.

I sat and waited, head bowed.

"Look at me," he commanded in a hollow voice that had me wondering what the hell we'd gone through these last few weeks that he could address me with such limited emotion when I was ready to be facedown in front of him, bowing to a king I never knew I would have to serve, but enjoying the servitude because it was him.

Donovan.

His dark eyes were trained on me for a few short seconds before he leaned back and crossed his arms. "You cooked."

"Yes."

"For me?"

"For us," I said before thinking. Wincing, I waited for the pain for the deserved punishment.

Instead, he stilled and then reached for my chin, tilting it toward him with his finger. "Us?"

I gulped, willing the tears to stay in. "I just thought..." I tried again. "I'm bored and figured I could help with..."

"You thought," he repeated slowly. "What? That I would magically fall in love with you the minute, you cooked me pasta?"

"No." I wanted to scream. "No, that's not what I—"

His smirk killed the next words I had. "I was kidding, pet. Thank you," he leaned forward and pressed a kiss to my mouth, murmuring, "for the food."

I wanted to swallow him whole. Exist in only a place where we could be together. No family. No politics.

Us.

Just us being us.

Like we were in that kitchen, but that wasn't my reality.

"You're bored." He pulled away from my mouth, contemplating what he was going to say next. "What can I do to fix your boredom, Juliet?"

My mouth dropped open. "You mean ... you would let me leave?"

He arched an intense eyebrow.

"No! Not like leave, leave, but off the premises?"

"I don't understand the question."

"I could leave and go to the mall or something?"

"This is about you wanting to go to the mall?"

"No, not really."

"Then how about you use your words and stop talking in circles. If you want something from me, then I expect to hear you address it, understood? I don't play games."

"But what if you don't like what I have to say?"

"Then I take you over my knee and spank your ass raw, but, pet..." He paused for a second. "We both know how much you like that."

I blushed, bowing my head.

"Juliet."

His gentle voice made me peer up at him.

"Try me."

I bit my bottom lip. "Okay."

He leaned back into his chair, arms folded over his broad chest, waiting. I had to shove away all the dirty thoughts I had of him in that moment, wanting my voice to be heard. I'd be lying if I said I wasn't internally flipping the fuck out.

"Pet, I'm waiting."

Before he could say anything, I exclaimed, "I'm nervous."

"Are you scared of me?"

"I don't want to make you upset."

"So what you're going to tell me will upset me?"

"I don't know."

He grinned in a devilish way. "Only one way to find out."

"Fine. I want a job."

At my request, he jerked back. "A job?"

"Yeah, you know. Something I can do for you."

"Something you can do for me? More than you already do?"

I smiled at his retort. "I'll do anything you want, Master."

"And look at that—when she wants something, she's polite and respectful."

I shrugged, hiding back my smile.

"What would you like to do for me?"

"I mean, I could help with things. Like Elaina, maybe?"

"Like Elaina?"

"Yes. She helps with the slaves, right? She helped with me."

"I see."

His grin was my undoing. God, I loved it when he smirked like that. I wished I could save them all for when I was sad, for when I missed Romeo, when I missed my old life, my old self, only to realize I wasn't the same anymore.

I wasn't me.

I was his.

Owned.

And I never wanted to go back to what once was. As sick as it made me, I never wanted to be well.

I metaphorically dumped the prescription for sanity the day he took me against the piano and laughed at the idea of ever returning to normal. I stayed as calm as I could, looking demure, folding my hands in my lap when all I wanted was to run around the room screaming in excitement.

Finally.

I said what I wanted.

"It's interesting you decided today was the day to tell me you wanted a job. Considering, I already decided you get to host the next auction. You'll need Elaina's help, of course, but you'll be able to decide the menu down to the first appetizer." He reached into his pocket and pulled out a key fob. "Also, I was late because I was out shopping for this."

"A key?" I took it in my hand, rubbing the Lamborghini symbol so much I was surprised it didn't rub completely off. "For what?"

"Your new car," he simply replied, standing to his feet. "I'd get going, by the way. You only have a week to prepare for the next auction, and Elaina needs help with the preparations."

Stunned, I looked down at my outfit. I was wearing a silk nightie since I had to be naked nearly twenty-four seven. My collar never came off.

"I need to go get ready."

"She wouldn't be surprised if you showed up like that." Donovan shrugged. "But do as you wish. I'm going to go take a shower."

Panic set in as he began to walk away.

Was he done with me? No longer interested? Why else would he be so accommodating?

The idea of him shoving me away had me ready to fall to my knees. I sucked in a breath. And another. Until all I was doing was trying to breathe.

Donovan grabbed my body and pulled me against him. "Shhh, pet, you're safe."

I clung to him, wrapping my arms around his neck so tightly it hurt.

"You wanted this," he reminded me. "And it's because of your reaction now that I'm giving it to you. Because you can't live without the pain or the pleasure. You can't live without your master, and now you know what it feels like when everything secure in your life looks like it's washing away." He pried his body from mine and kissed my forehead. "You need me as much as I need you—never forget it."

With that, he walked away.

I rubbed the key fob in my hand, realizing, maybe, this was more than a test. This was him giving me the space I needed to thrive.

Even if it killed him.

I quickly got ready, and he met me at the door, letting me know I could drive my new car; however, I must follow the ten guards he was sending with me. At that point, I didn't care if he had a hundred of them on my ass if it meant I could leave the estate by myself.

He told me Elaina was waiting for me at the other property, the one where Troy had hurt me, triggering my body to shiver at the memory.

If Donovan noticed my reaction, he didn't call me out on it. I knew he must have noticed; the man noticed everything.

I jumped into my new ride, ready to meet Elaina, only to get sidetracked by the gorgeous SUV and the small card and rose waiting for me on the passenger side.

"Yours," it read.

His.

I was his.

He was mine.

I sniffed the rose way too long and then started the vehicle.

Minutes later, I was smiling at myself in the rearview mirror of my new Lambo SUV, wondering how the hell he was even able to get one on such short notice.

Suddenly, my mind reminded me of all the times we'd traveled this road in my other car, with my family and friends. All the times I'd looked out the window and wished for purpose, something more, better. All the times I'd compared myself to my brother and everyone else in my powerful family, knowing I'd always come up short.

I frowned at the steering wheel, not even knowing I was taking the familiar exit until it was too late. I drove on autopilot, taking a right, then a left, a right, driving on for five miles until I was in front of the gates. It was ten thousand square feet. Huge. Had brick everywhere and a circular driveway. There was a special entrance in the front, a private entrance in the back. It used to be mine.

My family's.

The guards didn't get out of their vehicles. They stopped, watching and waiting. I exhaled, my fingers gripping the steering wheel like it was going to come off the car at any minute, and I had only one job—keep them there.

I didn't know how long I stared, but long enough to realize one thing. As confused as my mind was, my body knew. It worked on autopilot for me, driving away and toward the manor I was meeting Elaina at. The SUV in front of me once again led the way. In that moment, I didn't just choose Donovan.

In a way, I chose me.

CHAPTER EIGHTEEN

Romeo

Was my mind playing tricks on me?

I thought I saw a Lambo SUV driving away on the property. It was a vehicle I didn't recognize, and the only way anyone could enter through the gates of my family's estate was if they had a code. I felt it deep in my bones. Something wasn't right, and for the first time since my sister was taken, I had an unnerving suspicion that something was going on.

My life was consumed with trying to find her, only to come up empty. There was no trace of her, not one. It was like she'd disappeared into thin air. The motherfuckers who had taken her knew what they were doing, and I was beginning to think that we would never find my baby sister. The thought alone made me want to kill anyone in my presence. My temper was looming, and it wouldn't take much to push my buttons.

"Babe," Eden rasped, wrapping her arms around me. "You'll find her. I have full faith that you will find her."

I moved my lips across her shoulder. "You smell good enough to eat, Red." It was the nickname I'd been using for my wife for as long as I could remember.

Every time I thought about the fact that she could have been taken too, I wanted to kill the guard who was supposed to be protecting Juliet all over again.

"I love you. Get lost in me, Romeo."

I gripped onto her ass and wrapped her legs around my waist, doing exactly that. For the rest of the day, I found refuge in my wife and all the ways she always made me forget.

Juliet

I followed the guards and pulled in front of the property that still haunted my dreams. A knock sounded on my window, and I jumped and looked.

Troy stood there, blue eyes gleaming, pointing for me to roll down the window.

I hesitated and hit the down button.

His grin made my stomach churn, stating, "Elaina couldn't make it today, so I'll be showing you the ropes."

Shaking, I reached for my phone. The one that Donovan had given me that only worked for his number. I sent him a quick text.

All it said was Troy.

I had no idea how he'd take it, but I needed to at least send it to him to feel safe.

Troy opened the driver's side door and let me out, escorting me inside the daunting mansion. I'd been around money my entire life, but something about their business, their dynasty, made me nervous.

"So this is it," Troy emphasized, opening the double doors to the ballroom. "As you remember, every auction and or party takes place on this property, passed down from generation to generation."

I cringed at how close he was to me and took a step to the side, examining the open room like I hadn't been part of it just a few weeks before, wearing my collar, feeling hurt and exposed, playing for him but actually them.

I shuddered. "Is there a different theme each time?"

Troy paused before running a finger down my bare shoulder. "What a fantastic question… Yes, it depends on whoever's hosting, which means this time you get to choose since your master deemed you worthy."

I wanted to say I was always worthy, but I bit my tongue. "Interesting."

"Isn't it?" He grinned. "Come on, more to show you."

We walked from room to room until we were at the left wing of the mansion.

"What's back here?"

I would never forget the expression on his face while he opened the doors to a room that still had dried-up blood on the floor.

I gasped, my body shaking to the core. Following his lead, I walked in behind him. My eyes landed on a closet that had gashes in it like a knife was stabbed into the wood numerous times.

"Does Donovan own this place too?"

"Donovan, huh?"

Shit.

I abruptly corrected myself, "I mean, Master."

He eyed me skeptically. "This and many others—it's a family business, you know… The Society, the properties, the money—it's been in Donovan's family for a very long time. His father, God rest his soul." He watched me out of the corner of his eyes. "He believed in achieving self-actualization through this program, through The Society. What better way to achieve your best self than to look at all your pleasure and pain through someone else's eyes?"

My stomach tightened until I thought I was going to double over in pain.

"Oh." I swallowed. "That makes sense."

"Yes, well…" Troy continued to walk me through the room. "This property does hold a special place in Donovan's heart, especially this room."

Our eyes connected. "Why is that?"

"Oh, he didn't tell you?"

I shook my head. "Tell me what?"

All of a sudden, a familiar voice roared, "Nothing that fucking concerns you." Donovan emerged from the double doors, looking every bit the dominant master he was. His eyes locked on Troy. If glares could kill, Troy would be dead. "Where is Elaina?"

Relief hit my senses, not realizing that I needed to hear the words that Donovan didn't know Troy was with me. He didn't leave me alone with this sick bastard, and it was the reassurance I needed to think that I was different.

I wasn't just his slave.

His pet.

He did care about me.

"She didn't feel good, so she sent me to meet your pet instead. Why? Is that a problem?"

"I can handle it from here." He nodded toward the doors, dismissing him. "You can go."

Troy leaned forward and kissed my head. "Till next time, little one."

Donovan didn't move an inch, nor did he show any emotion. Despite me grimacing the instant I felt Troy's mouth on my scalp.

Right when he left, Donovan looked ready to burn the world down if need be.

For me?

"I'm sorry, Master."

His eyes now connected with mine. "What are you apologizing for?"

"For Troy."

He was in my face before I got his name out, grabbing my arm so I couldn't stumble back. "You don't ever apologize for that son of a bitch. Do you understand me?"

I nodded, bowing my head.

"Look at me."

I lifted my eyes, emotions in turmoil as I waited.

"That shouldn't be what you're apologizing for."

My eyes widened.

Of course, he would already know. The guards probably called him the second they followed me into my family's neighborhood.

"What do you think…" His voice soothed my soul, the way it caressed over me like silk. Yes, I would crawl back to him even if I could walk. It was about the feeling of looking up at him in adoration and worship, about knowing who you served.

My king.

Mine.

Master.

"…Your punishment should be?"

"W-what?" My head whipped back, nearly colliding with his chin. "For what?"

His eyes flashed. "For being tempted."

I sucked in a sharp breath. "But I didn't get out of the car."

"But you thought about it," he whispered in my ear from behind me, bracing my body with one arm while tugging my hair into a ponytail with the other. "Didn't you? Didn't you imagine and fantasize what would happen if you went home?"

"I am home," I responded quickly.

He jerked me against him. His arousal so present that a moan escaped my lips as he rubbed himself against my ass. "That's right," he growled. "I am your fucking home. I'll kill you before I let you forget it, so what is your punishment, pet?"

"I don't … I don't know." My mind was blank.

I couldn't even think of a proper punishment with him holding me like that, bracing me, keeping me safe when all day I'd felt fear.

"I'll decide then, yes?" he finally countered after a few heartbeats. "On your knees."

When I didn't move fast enough, he forced me to the hard ground, and my knees were the first thing to hit the floor. He didn't waver, basically tearing my clothes from my body until I was completely naked and staring up at him with only my collar.

His dark eyes stilled and then roamed across my skin, over and over again like a predatory caress. "Stay."

"What?" I asked.

"Stay," he repeated. "Until I'm ready for you, stay."

Tears burned my eyes, but I remained naked on my knees. Waiting for my master, waiting for my keeper, waiting to be released—and hating that the entire time, arousal dripped from every last inch of me.

For him.

For us.

For when the time came that he'd feed me one morsel of his touch, his taste, his scent. He was my jailor—me his prisoner—begging to be forgotten rather than set free because I could only be with my captor in my dreams.

Donovan

I knew there was a reason I put bodyguards on her. Not to keep her safe. No to keep her mine. It had nothing to do with actual safety but the fear of losing her to her own family—even to mine. When I saw her stop, I wondered if she would actually do it. Be able to leave me.

I had my answer in seconds.

I knew she was getting bored, and the time had come to proceed with the next steps of our relationship. If she wanted to work, I could grant her that. Her job would give her the illusion that she was being useful for something other than my pleasure and pain.

The nerve of that prick really did make me want to shoot him in between the eyes. I fantasized about it while I sped the entire drive to the property. Fully aware he wouldn't hurt her, he wasn't that fucking stupid. What he wanted to do was scare her, and by the look on her face when I arrived, he'd succeeded in doing so.

As soon as she saw me, her expression screamed it all. It shouted: own me, protect me, mark me—make him go away. I couldn't give that to her without punishment first for disobeying my orders, although I wanted to.

I needed to show her who the master was. After, I'd love her the only way I knew how, and I'd worship her in a way that ruined her the next morning and the days to follow.

She. Was. Mine.

I was hers.

Everything would set itself to rights again. Except, I couldn't do it, not with her kneeling in front of me, her pretty eyes lit up with tears, her swollen mouth begging for my cock, her pretty pussy gleaming, nearly pulsing with need.

I left her.

I went outside to collect myself and dialed his number.

He answered on the second ring. "Surprised it took this long…"

"Blindside me again with her, and I'll fucking kill you."

Never had my voice been so calm, never had my heart beat so fast, waiting for Troy's response.

A sigh.

A chuckle.

And then… "Sure, whatever you say, boss."

I growled, "I'm serious, Troy. Not this one. Not this time."

"Hey! I was just showing her the business. You're the one who took it upon yourself to include her in it."

I barked out a laugh. "Followed by a detailed show and tell of your dick? Right?"

"This is why we get along." He laughed. "Because you understand! Business is business, and we never bring anything personal into business, right, Donovan? We wouldn't want to make the same mistake your father did. You know, getting too attached. Man was almost unhinged before his untimely death; what was it again? An accidental—"

"Shut the fuck up!" I gripped the phone so hard I could swear my palm was bleeding. "Cross me again, and you'll know exactly how he died. Only this time, it will be you looking up at me in horror as you breathe your last breath."

Silence crackled through the phone, and the air was tense with it.

"Do your worst, Donovan, do your worst. And I'll do mine."

So he picked a side. It had always been about Troy and only Troy. He made it seem like he was rescuing me, saving me actually; instead, he was damning me and making plans in the process. Back then, I wasn't smart enough to see it. Recently, it took everything in my damn body not to kill him and take it all. He still owned a portion of our company. Which meant he still owned part of my past, and he wanted to dictate my future, a future where he thought he could have what was mine.

Never fucking happening.

I hung up, shoving the phone into my pocket as I returned to the room I hadn't walked into in who knew how long before this evening. Juliet knelt, waiting for me, chin tucked and eyes closed.

"Perfect," I whispered.

Her ass was so round, so ready for my hands to grip, her hair falling across her shoulders in the short cut I'd given her with the scissors I'd used. I took a minute. I never did that. I never hesitated.

But I did then.

For the first time, I wanted more than the pain. More than the pleasure. I wanted everything, and she was the only one I wanted it from.

"Juliet."

Her head jerked up, her eyes wide. "Y-yes?"

"Juliet." I reached out, my hand caressing her cheek before pulling her up to stand on her two feet. Gripping her face with both hands, I pressed my mouth to hers, devouring kiss after kiss, tasting her need, feeling my own. "Juliet." I bit down on her bottom lip.

I needed more.

Much more.

We pulled apart, both of us breathless as she stared me down, a nervous smile spread across her face.

"I know what I want my punishment to be, Master."

I arched an eyebrow.

"I want to touch you."

"So this punishment is for me?"

She blushed with a shy smile creeping. "I've never touched a man before, and the thought of touching you excites me, but it also terrifies me. You know you are kind of scary, right?"

Grinning, I remarked, "Kind of? And your mouth and pussy have touched me, pet."

"Right, but only your lips and your, you know."

"I don't know. Why don't you remind me?"

"Master…" She blushed profusely, and I found it arousing.

"You've had my cock in your mouth too many damn times to not be able to say the word to me, pet."

"Well, you can say it for the both of us." She beamed, looking fucking radiant. "Can that be my punishment? Please…"

"You know how much I love it when you beg me."

"Is that yes?"

"It's not a no." Before I could change my mind, I ordered, "Take off my shirt."

The surprised expression on her face was enough to drive any sane man crazy.

I wasn't sane.

Normal.

I was a fucking sociopath, and don't think for one second I wasn't or that I wasn't aware of it. On the contrary, I'd embraced it long ago. It was the only way I could survive in this seedy world. I took the good with the bad—though, there was more bad than good.

She was good.

Juliet was pure.

Innocent.

Naive.

She was the complete opposite of me, and part of her allure was that I corrupted the angel in my darkness. In my dungeon. In my hell. I had no fucking problem in doing so. I wasn't alone anymore—I had her.

With the devil on my side, I'd keep her forever.

Like a fallen angel sinning over and over again, I'd keep her.

Her fingers slowly raised toward the first button on my dress shirt, and little by little, she unbuttoned each one until it was fully opened and ready for her touch. Her eyes widened at the expanse of skin like she couldn't drink in enough of me. God, it was addicting, a sin I'd commit endlessly, making her fall for the villain, making her need me.

"Where do you want to touch me, pet?" Anticipation coursed through me like a shot of adrenaline; had I ever wanted anything more? No. Never.

Her gaze shifted toward my chest, and the first place she wanted the palm of her hand to touch was right over my godforsaken heart.

No one had touched me there except for my mother, always saying that as long as my heart was still beating, she could go on.

"How do you do that?" She gave me an awestruck expression.

"Do what?" I replied above a murmur, getting lost in the still of her eyes.

"Keep your heartbeat steady like that. How do you always stay calm in situations that cause you distress?"

I wanted to tell her she should know, knowing who her family was, what her past was. Instead, I was blatantly honest. "It's how I stay alive in a world that wants me dead."

"Does that include Troy?"

"I don't want to talk about him right now," I said quickly.

She was the first to break our trancelike state. Leaning in, she softly, tortuously kissed along my heart, letting her lips linger for a couple of seconds before she glided them down toward my stomach until she was on her knees.

Willingly.

In front of me.

Her stare asked if she could undo my belt and slacks, and I nodded. Carefully, she undid them both, and my cock stood at attention for her.

I wanted to see how far she would take this. How brave she'd be in a moment when I seemed so weak.

I didn't do gentle.

Soft.

I was rough in everything I did, especially fucking.

Once my dick was in her face, she licked from the head, down the shaft, and back up again. I groaned, feeling vulnerable that I was giving her all the control. I didn't do that either. This was a first for me, and I wasn't quite sure if it would be the last either.

I was torn.

Hard as hell.

Waiting for her to do as she pleased. This punishment was more for me than it was for her; that much was sure.

"Donovan," I heard her whisper, deep throating my cock again.

She knew what I liked; however, she was giving me what I wanted so achingly slow that my balls felt like they were about to explode.

It was so real.

So true.

So consuming.

She was right there with me.

If this was a dream, I didn't want to wake up. Not now, not ever. I felt her hand start to work me over as if she was making love to me with her mouth.

Up and down.

Twisting and turning.

In and out.

I was in her mouth and hands.

"Juliet, you're such a good girl. You're such a lovely pet," I praised, resisting the urge to grip onto the back of her head and thrust my dick to the furthest part of her throat.

Hard.

Eager.

Fast.

I stirred, focusing on how fucking breathtaking she looked, on her knees, serving me...

Her Master.

For now and forever. Never to be parted...

CHAPTER NINETEEN

Donovan

"You're so beautiful. Do you have any idea how beautiful you are?"

She moaned, vibrating my core with her mouth still wrapped around as much as she could take of my dick. Usually, I made her take all of me. She didn't have much of a gag reflex, and that was always a good trait to have, not that it mattered because, at the end of the day, she'd learn to take me.

Her eyes held so much emotion. Her sincere expression was almost hard to follow. I had always been so in tune with what her eyes shared with me, and at that moment, all I could see was love.

Devotion.

Sincerity.

My heart ached at the sight of her. So fucking submissive. Subservient. Wanting to only please me with whatever she could, in any way she could. There was no confusion on her behalf, and it was wreaking havoc on the pieces that were still left of me. I could physically feel her love, and it was an emotion I wanted to keep forever. Feeling it so much more than I could have ever imagined. Almost like I could touch it.

Smell it.

Bathe myself in it.

Like a final baptism, linking us together forever.

"Donovan, stop thinking." She lifted her hand to touch over my heart again.

This time it was beating faster.

Urgent.

Demanding.

Beating a mile a minute for only her. My control was gone. I wasn't sure if I'd given it over to her or if she'd just stolen it like a thief in the night—did it matter anyway? It was hers. I was hers. Always. Forever. Hers.

"Just feel me. Be here with me, just me and you," she whispered, sensing my apprehension.

I watched, caressing the side of her cheek with the back of my fingers as we stared into each other's eyes, seeing our truth, our tainted love, reflected back at us.

I wouldn't come.

I couldn't.

Not when she was being this delicate with me, but I didn't stop her from trying. I could tell her mouth was becoming sore, tender, and it was enough to drive me over the edge, knowing I was causing her distress.

Pain and pleasure, they went hand in hand for me.

I growled, shooting my seed to the back of her throat, and she didn't hesitate in swallowing every last drop of my come.

"Good girl."

Smiling, she wiped her mouth with the back of her hand. "We're not finished."

"Is that right?"

She nodded.

"I'm taking orders from you now?"

"Maybe. How does it feel?"

"Terrifying. Better hurry, pet. I don't know how much longer I'm going to play this game with you."

"Yes, Donovan." She stood with my help. Grabbing my hand, she led me to the bed on the other side of the room.

Juliet's eyes peered at the blood on the floor, but she quickly averted her stare back in front of her. She wanted to ask, but I wouldn't tell.

At least, not right now.

We arrived at the bed, and she awkwardly looked over at my face. "Can I undress you, Master?"

"Master, is it now? What happened to Donovan?" I tested her, peering at her wide-eyed expression, needing her more than air and hating that I was desperate for more.

"Do you want me to call you Donovan?"

"This is your punishment, pet. What would be worse for you?"

She bit her lower lip, shrugging. "Neither or."

Unable to identify what I felt about that, I changed the subject. "You can undress me, Juliet."

"Pet."

"Excuse me?"

"I like it when you call me pet." Her voice lowered while her eyes lifted, meeting my expression like an equal. My cock stirred. Damn it, she was perfect. Everything I needed, wanted, craved.

"Noted. Now undress me."

She did as she was told and placed her hands on my chest, trying to get me to sit on the edge of the mattress.

I did.

The little minx spread her legs over my lap and slowly sat on my dick, taking every last inch of me.

She let out a small gasp once I was fully inside of her, getting used to the size of my cock like she always had. Clearly determined, she wrapped her arms around my neck and began riding. This was the first time we ever had sex like this, and again, I didn't know if it would be the last.

And as she continued to ride me, I realized it couldn't be.

I wouldn't let it be.

This wasn't the last.

This was the last of many firsts.

And our forever.

She just didn't know it yet.

Juliet

I softly pecked his lips, kissing him in a way I never had before. Teasing him with the tip of my tongue, I outlined his mouth. My tongue sought out his, and he kept my speed. Allowing me to set the pace, it turned passionate, needy, heady. Taking what the other needed. There was something agonizing about the way we devoured each other's mouths.

Burning with fire.

In his flames, I found myself scorching in a blaze of glory. Deeper and deeper, we seared together. Further and further, we burned alive. Each of us pushing the other further until we were consumed by the hot flames as they licked across our sweaty skin.

I couldn't get enough of him, wanting more. Wanting everything. Trying to become one person, I kissed him as if our lives depended on it. My fingers glided across his face, his chest, his back. My greedy hands seemed to find a million different reasons to continue to touch, grab.

He didn't touch me, and I didn't understand why until I realized he was waiting for me to tell him he could. It was the funniest feeling to finally get what I thought I'd wanted for so long.

I was wrong.

I wanted his caress.

His rough, demanding hands.

His brutal assault.

His wicked words and commands.

I wanted to make love, and it was only then that I truly understood that we had. All this time, all those thrusts, all those orders…

We were making love.

In our own way.

It was fucked up.

But it was ours.

"Please, Donovan… Please touch me. Take me like you want." Not just like he wanted—like I needed. Like a person starved for one more caress, one more taste. I'd drink my fill until I was sick and overflowing with everything Donavon had.

"Is that the punishment you think you deserve, pet? My hands on you?"

"No," I coaxed in between kissing him.

Long.

Hard.

Insistent.

"Your touch is never a punishment, not even when you're making me bleed for you. I'm yours. Do what you please. Break me just to fix me. Please…"

Asking to be broken.

Fixed.

Only to be broken again.

I wanted this insane necessary shattering between us, and I was going crazy with it. Repeatedly the carousel spun, and I never wanted off the ride. He didn't have to be told twice. Harshly, he fondled my breasts, grazing around my nipples, cupping and kneading them in the palm of his hand.

"Master," I moaned in a low voice I didn't recognize.

I was flipped over, suddenly beneath him as he hovered above my body. In one forceful thrust, he propelled my body almost to the headboard until the wall shook like the pictures were about ready to fall from the force of our bodies joining.

Grabbing my chin, he claimed my mouth. His movements became erratic as he pounded into my core.

Over and over.

Again and again.

My eyes widened in pleasure, my back arching off the bed, letting him lap at my neck and breasts, nipping, sucking, licking. Leaving marks and bruises in his wake. I didn't want to move, enjoying the sensation of his everything as both pleasure and pain washed over me in a wave of ecstasy.

"You feel me inside you?" he groaned, reading my mind and making his way back up to my mouth.

"Yes…" I breathed out.

My arms reached around, pressing him flush against my body, wanting to feel his entire weight on top of me. His warmth consumed me as he hit all the right spots. His back muscles flexed with every thrust. Every push and pull. I couldn't get enough of him.

I needed.

Wanted.

Loved.

Craved.

Him.

He leaned his forehead against mine, looking deep into my eyes. Our mouths were parted, still touching, both of us panting profusely. With one hand, he snaked around to cup my ass, guiding my hips and angling them, making me take every last inch of his cock. With each devious thrust, he made silent promises.

Safe.

Secure.

Cherished.

He wasn't fucking me. He was making love to me in his own way. Memorizing my body. My need. My love. How he knew it was what I needed, I had no idea. But the way he looked at me said it all. He knew I loved him, he knew I'd fallen, he knew, and all I could do was continue to take the leap into his arms and pray he continued to catch me when I'd fall.

His heady movements were almost as pained as the glare in his eyes. All I felt was his heart over mine. His kisses deep within the depths of my soul, his strong hands and muscular body consuming me in ways I'd never experienced before. His once cold and icy demeanor was replaced with nothing but heat. It radiated off of him, absorbing into my overstimulated flesh.

He was mine.

I felt it in his breath.

In the beat of his heart.

In every single fiber of his being.

The good and bad.

Heaven and Hell.

Every part of him.

I took what I could get.

Every last ounce of him.

He started to come apart… Clawing. Gripping. Growling. Groaning. I climaxed down his cock. There was no time to recover before he flipped my body onto my stomach. Clutching onto my hair, he yanked and thrust back into me at the same time. Kissing my lips, he relentlessly pounded into my core once again.

Faster.

Harder.

Deeper.

He took me doggy style.

I didn't want him to stop. I wanted to stay like this until the end of time, with his body on top of mine. His demons. His torment. His fucked up jadedness.

Until there were no more breaths for me to take.

No more tears for me to make.

No more pain for me to feel.

Nothing. I'd be nothing after him. In the end, it didn't matter. Nothing did when I was with him.

He wasn't my villain.

He wasn't my monster.

This wasn't my happily ever after.

He was my master, and that was good enough for me.

CHAPTER TWENTY

Donovan

I couldn't stop.

Never wanted to.

I wasn't sure I could ever quit this woman, especially after feeling her body pulse around my cock, sucking me dry in a way I'd never experienced in my entire life.

I threw my head back like a fucking savage, a roar escaping through my parted lips as my eyes squeezed shut.

When I opened them, I froze.

She wasn't staring at me anymore.

She was staring at the door.

Face pale.

Lips parted.

Did I hurt her? Was she unhappy?

Panic swelled in my chest until she swallowed and looked back at me in what I could only decipher as a petrifying fear and shame.

Slowly I looked over my shoulder as Troy stood there, hand shoved down his pants, eyes locked onto both of us. "Don't let me stop you; I was just getting started."

Juliet scrambled to cover her body as tears filled her eyes.

I jerked a sheet from the bed and pulled it over her. Throwing on my slacks, I charged toward him in a rage that felt so powerful I was actually prepared to kill him, smiling while doing it.

"Get the fuck out!" I shoved him against the wall. "Now!"

He stumbled back. He was fit for his age, but he stood no chance against me. Calmly laughing, he buckled his pants up. "What? You used to like my observations, my corrections, my suggestions."

"I'm not asking again." I slammed the wall with my hand. A picture crashed to the floor as drywall flew all around us. The one of me and my mom. "Say another word, and I will kill you."

His smile was cruel, arrogant, punishing, locking eyes with me. "So you'd add another murder to your record? To this poor room?" He looked past me toward Juliet. "Scary, isn't he? When he's not controlled… Know you always have a safe space with me."

"Troy!" I roared. "Out! Now!"

"Hmm." He held up his hands in innocence, smile still in place. "It seems she is different… How very…"—his right eyebrow arched—"wonderful for you."

Bullshit.

I clenched my teeth as he backed away and left the room.

Everything came out of me in a rush, crumbling on top of my head. The memories. The pain.

The fear for her, then for Juliet.

Never for myself.

Troy was out of the room, but I could hear his footsteps and his last words. "Once a murderer, always a murderer…"

And I was gone.

Stuck in a world I'd purposefully forgotten. Stuck in a state of repeating history and needing a desperate escape.

"Donovan." Juliet was at my side in an instant as I stared at the wall, down at the blood still on the floor, then back at the wall.

It centered me.

Sometimes that was life, right? You had no choice but to subject yourself to memories that threatened to destroy you.

Relive them.

Watch them.

Own them.

Knowing that you would do nothing different in the end, that the outcome would be the same, and hating yourself when you realized that you brought more players into the game when all you wanted was a safe place.

An escape.

Pain.

Pleasure.

Her.

I shook my head.

"Donovan," she stressed my name again, the same way my mom used to with that same care, that same tenderness—concern. It killed me, burned my soul into fucking flames.

"You killed her!" I screamed. "You fucking killed her!"

Father threw his head back and laughed. "Oh, son, what else was I supposed to do with a pet I no longer needed? A product that was past its shelf life?"

I couldn't think.

Couldn't even speak.

I just saw the cat o' nine tails and gripped it in my hand, ready to strike. I wasn't a boy anymore hiding in the closet. I was a nineteen-year-old man, and this was my vengeance.

His smile grew. "Are you going to finally grow a set of fucking balls and hit me? You gonna make me bleed, son?" He held his hands out wide. "Do it." His nostrils flared. "I dare you."

"Donovan, where did you go? What's going on? Are you okay?" Juliet rocked me in her lap.

I recounted the memory to her in a harsh whisper. "It was dinner time."

"Okay, okay." She caressed my face with her knuckles, pulling the sheet over my body as I shivered. "What else, baby?"

Baby?

I would have scoffed, but I was frozen.

"It..." I started. "It was ... bad. He was different, like her death broke the last sane part of him, even though I watched it. I saw it. It was his fault. She was so pretty." I kept the tears in. "Her eyes were still open, and he made me close them. I prayed to a god who never saved us. To a family who she said would rescue us and nothing, nothing ... because everyone always lets you down, Juliet."

"Not everyone," she expressed quickly.

"Yes," I murmured. "Everyone."

My head fell back against her lap as I was brought back into the memory like I was right there in the present time.

My body might have been with Juliet.

However, my mind, heart, and soul were with my father.

"Whip me," he taunted. "Do it, just like I punished your mom. I'm so proud of you, Donovan, finally coming into yourself, the family business... HIT ME!"

So I did.

Again and again.

Enjoying the pleasure.

As I enjoyed inflicting pain.

I reached into the back of my jeans and pulled out a knife. The sickest part? He seemed to enjoy the fact that I was trying to threaten him, that I wanted to kill him; in the end, he was breaking me to become just like him.

Forget hugs.

He wanted blood.

So I would give it to him.

"Kill me. I fucking dare you to even try."

I counted.

I counted how many times the whip gripped into his skin, how many times it made the slick sound of skin getting churned.

One.

Two.

Three.

Four.

Five.

It was cathartic, counting because then I wasn't actually hitting him; no, it was his taunt, the numbers, the thought of my mom suffering the same fate almost a decade ago at that point.

A whip in one hand.

A knife in the other.

"You killed her!" I roared again.

"Shhhh." Juliet's tears fell against my cheeks. "Who killed who? Your father? Donovan, talk to me. It's okay; I'm here."

"And I'm there," I voiced hoarsely. "I'm still there ... one, two, three." I counted all over again. "It helps, you know ... the numbers. It's easier that way. Makes it less emotional when you count, when you think of it as inventory..." I shuddered in her lap. "He deserved it. Every stab. Every whip."

"But you didn't..." She held me tight. "You didn't deserve to be the witness, the executioner, the juror; you didn't, Donovan ... never—not then, not now."

"I did."

"You're wrong."

I sat up and stared her down. "I'm not your savior, Juliet. I couldn't save her. I refuse to save you."

She tilted her chin up. "Good, I've always believed a girl has to save herself. You aren't strong enough to save me, Donovan. I'm a woman. I know my worth. I know my strength. Despite the way I've been broken, I'm still free. The difference between us is that you aren't..."

Was she right?

"So..." She pressed a kiss to my mouth, soft, tender, loving, strong. "What happened next?"

I shook my head again, bringing myself back to a time when things were so dark I wondered if the sun even existed. Maybe in the past it simply didn't.

It was all dark.

All of it.

Ash raining down on my face, I looked into the heavens, smiled, and made my damning choice.

I grabbed the whip and rained holy hell down on my father until he collapsed onto the ground. Blood spewed out of his mouth, creating a river down his neck. I watched for a couple of seconds, consumed with the view in front of me.

Witnessing him bleeding out at my feet, I waited for it for so long, and it was finally upon me. I wanted to remember this moment for as long as I lived, cherish it, and carry it around with me. Gripping onto the knife, I shoved it into his wounded back.

A life for a life.

A kill for a kill.

He stole my mother's soul, and now I owned his.

His bloody smile was the last thing I saw before he revealed, "She's not even your mother, you fucking bastard."

Just like a Phoenix rose above his ashes, the monster created rose up above the river of blood and claimed his crown—his throne, his legacy.

"I didn't think you had it in you," Troy announced from the doorway.

Paralyzed, I couldn't even turn around. "How much did you see?"

"All of it," he snapped.

"Is it true?"

"Can you handle it?"

I shot around, staring deep into his beady eyes. "Is it fucking true, Troy?"

He held his hands up in a surrendering gesture. "I'm just the messenger, Donovan."

"Answer my question," I clenched out, my jaw tight as all hell. "Is. It. True?"

He shrugged. "She was your mother in every way that mattered."

I jerked back, stunned by his revelation. "Where is she then?"

"Who?"

"Stop playing your damn games! Where. Is. She?"

"Eh." He pushed off the doorframe. "She died giving birth to you."

My eyes widened. "How can this be?"

"You should be grateful. At least she didn't have to endure your father's recklessness like the slave who raised you as her own. She loved you, Donovan; that much we both know."

"Troy—"

"No, no, no, the question and answer portion of tonight is now over. We have more important things to discuss."

"Which are?"

"That you just proved to me that you were always better than your father and that mostly"—he moved toward me and pried the whip from my hands—"you need pain just as much as he did." Blood from the whip dripped across his fingertips. "Maybe even more than I could have possibly imagined. You need the balance; you need me." He dropped the whip and put both hands on my shoulders. "We'll continue this empire together, with you by my side." He shook his head at my father's dead body. "Son, we'll conquer the world." He abruptly stepped back. "I'll clean this up. You go take a shower and think about things. We have a lot of work in our future, but first." He cleaned off his hands and pulled out his cell phone, barking into it, "Send her in."

"Her?" I repeated, stunned stupid, in shock, afraid, lost. "Who is she?"

His smile revealed white capped teeth. "Yours, she's yours... Your first. Do enjoy taming your pet, Donovan. It might be the only way you can sleep tonight, and don't worry—she likes the pain."

A gorgeous woman stepped into the room.

She had a slinky black dress on and immediately fell to her knees, shoes off, hands open, waiting for me.

And like a drug, I went to her.

Needing her touch. Needing to punish her the way I was punished. Needing ownership.

Pain.

Loss.

Screams.

I gripped her by the hair and exclaimed, "Who am I?"

Her eyes dilated as she replied, "Master."

Juliet

He was shaking.

Did he even realize it? The way he clung to me?

"Master," he repeated from his panicked memory. "Now you

know… He killed my mother, and I paid him back in the same kindness. Troy saw." He sat up, facing me on the floor. "He saw, and he took me under his wing. Our business has always been this, but Troy…" He hesitated. "He's not the same as me. He's cruel, punishing, and he'd kill me to get to you."

"You're afraid," I said calmly. "Of turning into him."

"I fucking am him!"

"No." I was ready to slap him. "You aren't. You're controlled. You're loving. You know the boundaries. Maybe at first, I didn't see that, but now I do. I—" I almost confessed. "I see you, Donovan. I see you."

"Impossible." His voice cracked. "I stole you. All you see is what I want you to see."

"Had you given me a chance," I uttered softly. "I would have begged to be stolen by my monster, my villain. I would have tied myself up and opened wide for your taste, would have spread my legs and cried for the pleasure only you could give me, would have crawled across a floor just to serve my master. I would have—"

His kiss was sudden.

Painful.

Raw.

Mine.

Our tongues tangled as he pushed me back against the floor, hovering over me, his body weighing me down in such sweet surrender I wanted to cry. "Yes."

"Yes," he repeated. "Mine, all mine."

"Always," I agreed while he kissed down my neck.

He paused, his breath coming out in short pants and pinning me there. "I'll never let anything happen to you."

"I know that."

"I keep this estate to remember." His dark eyes met mine. "To never become him; no matter how much I need—to stay me."

I leaned up and kissed him across the mouth, setting my lips against his. "She'd be proud of you, Donovan."

"She wasn't even mine."

"She was in the ways that counted."

Our foreheads touched.

I didn't know how long we stayed like that until my stomach started growling.

With a sexy smile I hadn't seen from him ever. Donovan stood and pulled me to my feet. "Shall I feed my pet?"

"As long as it's not in a bowl," I joked.

He burst out laughing, pulling me into his arms. "Aw, pet, it would be my honor to serve…"

An hour later, he was looking at me while I ate.

"Aren't you hungry?" I devoured the snack he'd made for us, finally looking up as he watched me eat. "What? Is something on my face?"

He scoffed out a chuckle. "Would fucking kill to have you on my face."

I shot him a look. "Do you only think about sex?"

"Yes." He reached out and grabbed my chair, jerking it closer until our knees were intertwined. We were sitting outside, watching the gorgeous Seattle night sky. "Sex and you. Always. Every second. Every day."

I couldn't resist. "So, are all your pets like this?"

"Do you see any other pets?"

"No, but—"

"You're mine." He grabbed my fork and put a piece of fruit into my mouth. "Serve me during the day, then let me serve you during the night. Let me worship you while you submit so perfectly; doesn't that sound like the best ending to every fairy tale?"

"Servitude."

"What better way to show your devotion than on your knees? What better way for me to show my adoration than bringing you to them?"

I found myself smiling. "Somehow, that was the sweetest thing you've ever said to me." I ate the bite, leaning in. "I promise to always wait for you on my knees if you swear to keep me, own me, honor me—while you stand."

His smile was no longer cruel. It was beautiful, like seeing the ocean for the first time, like losing yourself then finding yourself again.

"You say I'm yours. But you're just as much mine, aren't you?"

He was quiet.

Too quiet.

All of a sudden, I was in his lap with his lips caressing my collarbone.

"Where else would I be? Then with you? When the world is chaotic, I'll be calm. When you have nowhere to turn, I'll be your home. When you think you're lost and afraid, let me be your map. I'm done, Juliet. I have so much to tell you, but I'm done—finished. This is it. You're my crescendo after a lifetime of playing." He pulled me in for a hug, his lips hot on my ear. "You're my finale."

I exhaled against his body, feeling him everywhere, too relieved to say anything but, "Don't forget…"

"I could never forget you."

"Then don't let me go."

"Never."

"I think…" I wrapped my arms around his neck. "I think I was yours before I even knew it."

He shuddered.

No more words were spoken. I enjoyed the moment in his arms.

Warm.

Safe.

Free.

I had no idea that it would be fleeting, this feeling. When you live with the villain, you never suspect horror. Although, it was there. Around the corner.

Lurking.

Waiting to strike.

And we were both too wrapped up in our broken fairytale to see it until it was too late.

CHAPTER TWENTY-ONE

Donovan

One Week Later

"Keep your phone on you, no matter what." I leaned into the SUV and warned Juliet for the tenth time as she put on her Ray-Bans and grinned at me like I was some sort of parent firing off all the rules for going off on their own.

Things had been tense between Troy and me.

She didn't know. I didn't want to involve her, but he'd been speaking to the board, telling them complete bullshit but also trying to convince them that he should have a heavier hand in the business.

My business.

The hell handed down by my father.

I always suspected him. I just never knew he would do it so blatantly in front of my eyes. It didn't help that he'd visited again a few days ago and told Juliet how beautiful she looked in front of Elaina.

Sometimes I hated him—more than I hated myself, which was saying a lot. And now Juliet was going out and helping with the next auction, meeting with Elaina, going out into the world I wanted to shield her from. I couldn't keep her in her golden cage forever, as much as I wanted to. The only peace I had was that she was surrounded by guards.

Juliet shot me a grin.

I looked away.

"Promise, Master."

My head shot back, my dick hardening. "You did that on purpose."

"Maybe I just like you that way."

I growled and jerked open the car door. I leaned across the console, unbuckled her seatbelt, and tapped her breasts lightly before reaching my hand between her thighs.

Her thong was soaked.

"Mmmmm." I gripped the thin fabric and tore it from her body. "Don't think you deserve these today."

"Dono—"

I glared.

"M-master." Her lips pressed together in a thin line. "I'm working, though…"

"Yes." I bit down on her bottom lip. "You are, and all day as you help with the auction, you'll remember my hand between your thighs, my fingers playing you the way you play the piano for me. You'll remember." I shoved a finger inside her heat. "You'll think of me until it hurts until you can't wait to come home and find"—I hooked my finger and then added another—"relief…"

"Master!" Her moan was both my heaven and my hell. "Please…"

"You argued, you teased, you taunted." I pulled my hand back and licked each finger. "So I'll do the same, just in case you forget who holds the keys to this kingdom."

"You," she rasped. "You, you, you, you—"

Her body arched so nicely.

I realized my control hadn't just snapped.

It was gone.

In an instant, I was out of the SUV.

Walking around to the driver's side, I yanked her door open. She stumbled against me as I slammed her against the side of the vehicle, lifting her skirt and needing to feel her to know she was mine. I hiked her silky dress up to her hips, and she undid my belt and pants, gripping me and freeing my cock.

Pain pounded into me. So sensitive, her grip so hard.

"Please." She squirmed against me, trapped, my prey.

I thrust into her in one smooth movement, my body nearly collapsing from the pleasure of her soft cries, of the way she tried to suck me in deeper, harder.

Anyone could see us.

I didn't give a shit.

I was home.

Even if I would never admit it out loud.

I pumped into her, my movements frenzied and desperate. For the first time in my life, they weren't planned or calculated, and it was all because of my Juliet.

Play for me.

Play for me.

Play for me.

Our bodies slapped against one another, then slowed, moving like a symphony, an orchestra, plucking the strings in a movement that made you pause, that made you wonder if there was a higher power. It made you question everything.

Your existence.

Your meaning.

She screamed out my name, not realizing I was already worshipping hers as it fell from my lips.

"Donovan…"

"Juliet." I pulled her dress down, straightened my collared shirt, and wiped between her thighs, soaking in the wetness, soaking in us, and wanting to make a damn trophy over it. "Stay safe. Keep your phone on you."

Her smile was satisfied. I put that there. "I promise."

"Good."

"Good." She leaned up and kissed me across the mouth. "I love…" She hesitated for a moment. "You, I do love you, Donovan, Master. Mine."

Stunned, I watched her get into the SUV and drive off.

And like the perverted motherfucker that I was, I looked down at my dirty shirt, inhaled, and smiled.

Juliet

When I walked into the house, my cheeks profusely blushed, remembering what happened the last time I was there a week ago.

I couldn't describe the emotions that Donovan stirred inside of me. For the first time in my life, I was happy.

Truly.

Unbelievably.

Happy.

I'd been wanting to tell him I loved him, and I was waiting for the right time to confess those three words. There was something about the way he looked at me that there was no stopping them from falling from my lips. I didn't expect him to say them back; he honestly didn't have to.

I felt his love.

Taking a deep breath, I walked into the room where Elaina would be waiting for me. She was already there, standing by the table that had all her makeup on it for the slaves to make over.

"You're late."

"I know. I'm so sorry." *Could she tell I was walking funny?* That I hated the emptiness between my thighs—the emptiness he'd left there.

She eyed my body up and down. "That's Donovan, having to fuck you before he leaves you alone for a minute."

I stopped dead in my tracks. *Was it that obvious?*

"Your hair is a mess, your dress is wrinkled, your eyeliner is smudged, and from the looks of it, you're not wearing any panties. If that doesn't scream freshly fucked, then I don't know what does."

Subconsciously, I straightened out my dress and tucked the unruly strands of my hair behind my ears.

"No, don't compose yourself, Juliet. We're in the business of selling sex, and—" she gestured to me "—what better way of getting our point across when you're radiating heat. They can smell it on you."

"But I'm Donovan's."

She smiled, big and wide, and I couldn't tell if that was a good or bad thing.

"Of course, darling. He'd never let anything happen to you; it's his number one priority as your master, and trust me when I say—you're different than his pets from the past. He'd actually die for you."

Unable to hold back, I blurted, "How does this work for you? I mean … with Troy. You're his wife, right?"

"It has a nice ring to it, doesn't it? *His wife.* I used to want nothing more than to have that title until I realized it doesn't mean one damn thing to him. It's just two words, like his slave, but forever."

"Does slave not mean forever?"

"In your case, it does."

"Oh…"

"Go ahead, ask your questions."

Should I? Could I? Was this another test?

"Your master wouldn't have sent you to me if he didn't already know that you'd be a curious little kitten. There isn't anything that I don't know, Juliet. You may as well ask. This may be the only chance you get."

"Have you … are you … is there a past between you and Donovan?"

She smirked. "I knew you'd start there given our relationship and the way he treats me, but no, pet. It's never been that way between us."

"Can I ask why?"

"I'm Troy's, and unlike him, there are boundaries that even Donovan won't break."

"Does that mean you wish he would have?" I wondered out loud, truly curious.

She finally shook her head after a few tense seconds. "No, he's not my type."

Reassurance washed over me. Elaina might have been older than I was, but she was still stunning.

"Now, is that it?" She clasped her hands in front of her.

I so desperately craved to ask her why Donovan took me, why he chose me; however, I couldn't form the words.

Not for one second.

"Sometimes being alive is better than being dead. We couldn't save your moth"—

she corrected herself—"his mother, so he's doing the best he can."

I opened my mouth to reply.

"We need to get the slaves ready." With that, she turned and started walking toward the door. "I'll be right back."

What did she mean by that? My mother?

I wasn't stupid.

My feet moved on their own accord, following after her. Except, as soon as I opened the door…

For the second time in my life, everything went pitch black.

Donovan

Elaina didn't have to tell me. When I walked into the estate, I felt it. The expression on her face was simply confirmation of what I had to do. I didn't want it to come to this. Never did I think it was going to. Which was only my fault; I should have known better.

Villains didn't get happily ever after's.

Not yesterday.

Not today.

Not tomorrow.

I was damned.

Swallowing my pride, I did what I had to do to save her.

Even if it meant the heroes killed me in the end.

CHAPTER TWENTY-TWO

Donovan

I drove up to the gates of Hell, literally. And just like the Devil, they didn't want me there either. The gates opened, and before I could hit the gas pedal, my SUV was surrounded by guards holding me at gunpoint.

I took a look around, deciding long ago that I would meet my maker at the hands of one of my enemies. Unfazed by what was happening, I opened the door and stepped out in plain sight. Standing tall and proud, I snidely smiled, leisurely glancing down at all the red laser marks that were now placed over my body from the artillery they were holding. Grinning, I slowly gazed up through the slits of my eyes. I waited a few seconds before taking the backs of my fingers and wiping away their target as if they were nothing but specks of dust.

Mocking them.

My stare shifted toward the hero, hauling ass out of the estate. Once the Mafia Casanova was in my face, he didn't waver.

Not that I ever expected him to.

Romeo

"What the fuck are you doing here?"

He didn't miss a beat. "Troy took her."

I glared at him, simply questioning, "But who took her first?"

He eyed me skeptically, arching an eyebrow. "It doesn't matter when someone as sadistic as him has her, and that's where your concern needs to lie right now."

I resisted the urge to fuck him up. "So you're here as what? Her captor or her savior?"

His jaw tightened. "Both."

I lunged at him, only to be held back by my father's men.

"Romeo!" he roared, rushing over to stand by my side. With his hand on my shoulder, he demanded, "Stand the fuck down."

My seething glare shot to my father's calm one, trying to listen even though every bone in my body struggled to follow his orders.

The son of a bitch didn't care in the least that I wanted to tear him to shreds. He knew I was aware of who he was and what he did for a living. If I could even call it that, living.

"Was she here? A week ago? Was she on this property?"

"If you're asking me those questions, then you already know the answers."

He was more like a death sentence for any woman who came in contact with him. Thinking of my baby sister at his mercy made my blood fucking sear. I always knew there was a chance for him to retaliate, but I never imagined it would be with Juliet.

How naive am I?

"Do you know what he's into?" Dad questioned while I held on by a very thin thread.

"I can imagine," he acknowledged, watching as my father pulled out his phone.

Picture after picture, lifeless body after lifeless body appeared on the screen.

If this motherfucker was surprised, he didn't show it. He was a blank canvas of emotion. Where I was ready to attack like a guard dog, he was ready to strike like the snake he was.

"This is what your business partner has been doing since before your piece of shit father killed your mother in front of your eyes."

He cocked his head to my father's statement. "And yet you never came back for me, but I wasn't her blood, was I?"

My heart pounded against my chest.

Louder and louder.

Faster and faster.

I exploded.

"Does Juliet know the truth?"

His gaze locked with mine, and I didn't realize I was holding in a breath until he simply shook his head and stated, "Not yet."

hhhhh!" I screamed bloody murder, jolting awake.

My head was throbbing, and the familiar pain was like coming home to Donovan when I first woke up on the piano in my old bedroom.

With wide eyes, my body propelled forward from the force of Troy's whip hitting my stomach.

"Stop! Please stop!" I begged, not caring that I sounded so weak.

He didn't; instead, he struck my chest, my legs, and the side of my neck. Blood immediately poured out of my flesh, staining my dress. I was shocked he'd left me clothed, and I wasn't naked, shouting for mercy.

I was sweating profusely.

Shaking.

Panting.

Was this what dying felt like? Was this what Donovan's mother felt?

"Well, well, well, look who finally decided to grace me with her presence. Did you take a nice nap, sleeping beauty?"

Whip to my inner thigh.

To the other one.

To the top of my mound.

"No more! Please, Troy, no more!"

"MASTER!" he yelled as the tail of the whip slammed against my cheek. "You call me Master! You're my slave now!"

I refused. He'd kill me before I ever addressed him as anything other than a psychopath.

"NEVER!"

The whip hit the same spot on my stomach, and I almost threw up from the rip-roaring pain, reminding myself that I could live through this.

He'd come for me.

I knew it like I knew my name.

Pet.

My head hung by my chest. I was exhausted, and he had only just started beating my flesh. I realized I was tied to the same cross he'd beat me on the last time.

"Juliet…" he sang in the creepiest voice I'd ever heard in all my life.

It was one of those tones that you heard in a horror movie, triggering the hair on your arms to stand straight up. Fear creeped up my spine, becoming a part of me.

Like Donovan.

My master.

"Let's play a game, shall we? I just love playing games. What do you think? Will you play for me, pet?"

He was using Donovan's words to mess with my head.

"Fuck you."

My head whooshed back from the force of his blow to the side of my face. I slowly turned my head around, glaring at him through the slits of my eyes, acting as if my cheek wasn't on fire. "You hit like a bitch." I spit blood on his face, and it landed near his mouth.

He viciously smiled, sticking out his tongue and licking it off.

"You taste good enough to eat. What do you think, pet? Do you want me down on my knees, devouring your pretty pink pussy?"

"Donovan will kill you if you touch me." *But would I be alive to see it?* My chest ached almost more than my body.

"Donovan and I have shared many slaves. Where do you think he learned everything he knows? I taught him how to touch, how to lick, how to fuck and beat women into submission."

"He's nothing like you," I spat.

"On the contrary—he's worse than me. I wasn't the one who killed my own father."

"That monster deserved to die. He should have done it sooner."

He rolled his eyes, gripping onto my mouth. "I thought you were smarter than you looked. The apple doesn't fall far from the tree, and Donovan is the spitting image of his father. Trust me, little one. I've seen what he's capable of. He stole you, didn't he? Mafia princess to the Sinacore family."

I swallowed hard and let go, but not before he licked off the blood from the gash on my cheek he'd just inflicted.

"You're such a pretty girl, much prettier than your mother was at your age."

I jerked back. "You know my mother?"

He smiled, reminding me of a Cheshire cat. "*Knew.* I knew your mother."

"What does that mean? Is my mother here too? Did you take her too, you fucking demonic asshole!"

He roughly pinched my cheeks, causing my lips to pucker. He crashed his mouth into mine with so much passion I thought he was going to rip my face off. Finally, he released me with a loud smack from his lips, pulling back to look me in the eyes as he licked more blood away.

"What do you want?" I gritted out, holding back the bile rising in my throat.

"What do I want? Hmmm…" he hummed. "I want a lot of things.

But first, I want to be the one to break you by telling you the truth about who you really are."

"Like I would believe anything you say."

"I'm a lot of things, but I'm not a liar. Let's see … where should I start? From the beginning, I suppose, right? It's always best to begin there."

I didn't stop him, and God help me, I wanted to know what he had to share.

Hit to my chest.

To my stomach.

To my leg.

"Ahhhhhh!"

"Yes! Scream all you want! No one can hear you, and no one's coming for you like no one came for your mother!"

"What?" I asked through the agony I was feeling.

"You heard me. No one cared enough to save her life. Your family didn't have to; they already had you. She gave you up willingly."

My eyebrows lowered. "Gave me up? What the hell are you talking about?"

"Your daddy…" he sang again in a high-pitched tone. "He couldn't keep his dick in his pants, and one night during an auction, Donovan's father shared your real mother with him."

"What?! No! No! No!"

"Yes! Yes! Yes! You're a fucking bastard! Your mom was Donovan's father's slave for twenty-two years, and when she wound up pregnant, she begged, pleaded, on her hands and knees to her Master to not make her get rid of you. So Donovan's father did the next best thing—he made a deal with your daddy. The Sinacores turned a blind eye to what we were doing in our business, and they got to raise you instead. With the woman you've believed to be your mother all these years when she's not. Your mother was a slave who couldn't suck cock to save her life, but that's not why he killed her."

My winded stare found his sadistic one. He was getting off on this, on breaking me.

They lied.

All this time, my whole life was nothing but a lie.

"He killed her because your mommy wasn't very bright, and she decided to take it upon herself to try to gain her freedom on her own. When Donovan was ten years old, she sought out your daddy to help her and Donovan escape from the only life she'd ever known. How poetic, right?"

I sucked in a breath. My heart was shattering into a million pieces.

"Why do you think your family has made it their mission to stop human trafficking? They weren't doing it for any other reason than to clear their fucking conscience. Your old man is a smart fucker; he knew Donovan's father would find out what she was plotting. In my opinion, he signed her death certificate long before Donovan's dad walked into that room and made Donovan hold that cat o' nine tails that ultimately killed her. Your mom's blood is on your father's hands."

Troy slammed my head into the metal X behind me as hard as he could, and instantly I saw stars. He knocked the wind right out of my lungs from the impact and his might alone. With a death grip over my windpipe, he pinned me against the X, not allowing me to properly breathe and catch my bearings.

My chest heaved, and my eyes watered, gasping for air that wasn't available for the taking. All the blood draining from my face, down to my lips that trembled with the instinctual desire to fall apart.

So much hurt.

Lies.

Betrayal.

"Now you know why Donovan had you kidnapped." He leaned in close to my lips. "You play the piano just like her. How fucking sick, right? To teach you her only talent as if they wanted her soul to live on through you. You're nothing more than a pretty doll that he puts on his shelf to show the world that you belong to him. Do you understand now? Are you seeing things clearly? More accurately? Did I paint the picture you wanted, pet?"

I wanted to know why Donovan chose me and now I knew the truth, and it was like dying with Troy's hand over my neck.

"For nine years, nine fucking years, Donovan's father taught him the ropes, showed him what it was like to be a master, own a slave, have a pet. Until Donovan turned nineteen years old and decided it was time to make his old man pay for his sins, for your mother's untimely death," he seethed into my ear, his hard cock pressed against my core. "Do you feel me, Juliet?" He let go of my neck to rip my dress. "Because now it's time to show you who's your real master with my dick deep inside of you. What better way to end this fucked up fairy tale you've created in your own head than to have my seed grow in your stomach. Proving to Donovan and your father who you truly belong to."

"NO!" I acted on pure impulse, banging my head into his nose as hard as I possibly could. Blood immediately flew from his nostrils while his body propelled back from the impact of my blow.

"You're going to pay for that, pet! It's time to make you lick my blood!" He lunged forward, and I tightly shut my eyes, turning my head into the X. Trying to get away from him. To hide.

Everything that proceeded next was in slow motion.

The doors to wherever we were slammed open.

Instantaneously, my eyes flew open and locked with my villain.

My hero.

I'd never forget the look in Donovan's smoldering glare as he took in my battered face, my bleeding body, trailing down to the rip in my dress that was barely covering my core. It was that exact moment we were both held captive by this psychopath's wrath.

The next few seconds played out in my mind resembling a reel from a classic movie. The glimpses of the black and white pictures were present as the current day, even though the stills were blurred, confusing, and utterly compelling. Nevertheless, we would never be the same again.

It was a memory neither one of us would ever forget, even if we wanted to, even if we hoped, even if we prayed, they were permanent. Exactly like his past. Troy was right—this wasn't a fairy tale. It was a nightmare I wanted to wake up from.

Except when I'd wake up, I'd be alone.

My villain would vanish like a thief in the night, stealing my heart and soul with him. I wouldn't be the same woman I was after this, and maybe that was his plan all along.

To set me free, even if it meant … I was lost without him.

CHAPTER TWENTY-THREE

Donovan

"Why?" Romeo asked as we pulled in front of the mansion. "Why not just let him kill her? You sadistic fucks are all the same."

I clenched my fists. "Don't talk shit you'll have to clean up later, Romeo. You fucked while killing, and you think you have the right to judge me?"

"Enough of this," Romeo's father barked out. "We're here for one thing and one thing only, to get my daughter back. Understand me?"

We nodded.

I held my hand toward Romeo after we got out of the car.

He stared at it, looking up at me. "What?"

"I don't have my gun on me, so I need one of yours."

His smirk made me want to smack him across the face then run him over with my car.

"I think I have a wooden one in the back. Maybe if you throw it hard enough, you'll—"

"Romeo!" Old man Sinacore sighed. "Give him one of yours, so we can get this business over with." His expression hardened. "Should have dealt with this shit a long time ago."

Romeo breathed deeply, handing me one of his Glocks before going to the trunk and pulling out two more and then shoving them into the back of his pants along with a sharp-looking knife.

Guess even heroes had their favorite toys.

I made the right choice.

In going to them.

In exposing myself as the true villain.

In confessing.

I had to think, as we walked up the steps and into the mansion, that in the end, I did good, and I did it all for her.

My Juliet.

It felt like my body was moving through a thick fog, walking in slow motion down the hall. My hand was heavy as I held the gun in my right hand.

But my thoughts were clear.

Get her out.

Get her safe.

Get her away from the bad guys—even if that meant I was getting her away from me.

A sudden pain attacked my chest, then spread outward and down my limbs until my entire body was heavy as sand.

"Where would he be?" Romeo asked, his eyes wild, glaring through the corridor at all the different rooms.

I stopped in front of the one Troy used to love to play in, knowing in my gut this was where he was. I kicked open the door and rushed in with both men at my sides.

Juliet looked up, scared. Her skin was marred from head to toe with blood, and chunks of flesh were missing from her thighs and chest.

Her right eye was completely swollen shut, her lips bloody, cheeks bruised.

He'd broken her body.

So I would break his now.

"You sick son of a bitch!" I roared.

"Oh." Troy looked over his shoulder. "You brought your own playdate."

"Get the fuck away from her," I said in a lethal tone. "Now!"

Troy finally turned and looked at the men, slightly paling at the sight of one of the most formidable mafia families staring him down with guns pointed in between his eyes.

"You really think you can take me down?" Troy laughed. "I have connections. I know every senator in—"

Romeo shot at his leg, nearly taking it off. "That's what I think about your fucking connections."

I laid my hand out in front of him. If anyone was going to kill this motherfucker it was going to be me.

Tears ran down Juliet's cheeks.

I mouthed, "Are you okay?"

She nodded slowly.

My angel.

Broken.

Bloody.

While the devil stood by and watched it happen.

Troy was still screaming out in misery when I ran up behind him, catching him by surprise, and grabbed the cat o' nine tails from his hands. I didn't waste one more second of what I came to do, what I'd hoped for, what I'd prayed for in who knew how long.

To have his blood on my hands.

"Donovan—"

Not allowing another moment to go by, I started raining holy hell all over Troy's body, forcing him to his knees.

"You fucking hit her," I seethed. "Now it's my turn to hit you!" I slammed the whip down across his back. "You made her bleed, and I'll steal every ounce of blood you have left! You made her fucking scream, cry, and scarred her perfect skin for you!" I crashed it down so hard it took away chunks of skin from his forearms. "And I'll make your body unrecognizable. Wishing you were never born!"

Troy held his arms up, blocking each strike, making it easy to take more and more of his skin, pouring out more and more blood, until a hand came back and grabbed my wrist.

"You'll kill him."

I glared back at Romeo, stressing, "Good."

His eyes widened.

"Give me your knife."

Without hesitation, he handed it over, and I grabbed Troy by the hair, exposing his throat, and drove the knife straight into his chest, all the way to the hilt.

"My boy." A tear slid down Troy's cheek. "So proud, so, very, very." He smiled through the blood oozing from his mouth. "Proud."

He fell in a gory heap to the floor.

Cursing me one last time, even in his death, as if I had somehow given him a hero's burial. In his eyes I'd killed him, taken him out in a reign of final glory without even realizing it.

Hating myself more for giving him exactly what he wanted.

Letting my eyes linger on his dead body for far too long, I wanted to remember this moment and look back on it when I needed to smile, to stay calm, to find peace in a world that only caused distress and disorder. Once I was finished, I spit in his face, resisting the urge to piss on it instead.

Quickly, I looked toward Juliet while her father was undoing the ropes on her wrists before helping her off the X. She stumbled on her feet, strangling a cry as she ran past me, directly into Romeo's arms and then her father's.

In the end, the good guys won, and the bad guys didn't.

One of us was on the ground, in a pool of his own blood, while the other had just watched his everything run past him and into her real hero's arms—her brother, her father—her family.

"I missed you so much, sweetheart." Romeo kissed her forehead.

"We need to get you looked at." Her father cupped her chin tenderly. Not aggressively.

There was no fear in their touch, despite the fact that they were trained killers; there was only care, love, security, warmth.

The only thing I could compare it to was the way I had begun to feel when Juliet looked at me, when she touched me, and the way my mother's music used to wrap itself around me, setting me free.

Setting. Me. Free.

"It's finished." I found myself saying, my voice cracked. I might as well have crashed against the floor like Troy.

I knew I was different than him.

But it didn't change the fact that I'd stolen her away from them.

Kept her for myself.

Hurt her for my pleasure.

Only to leave her behind.

"Take her home," I added, nodding at them to do as I demanded.

Needed.

Wanted.

Despite feeling like I was going to die.

Romeo froze; his expression went from shocked to grave as Juliet collapsed against him, bursting into tears.

"Donovan?"

I couldn't look at her. "It's what's best. Take her."

"But … I don't understand." Tears streamed with blood down her face, mixing with our tainted love story and tragic end. "You're my home, Donovan—Master—"

I flinched when she fell to her bloody knees and wrapped her arms around my legs.

"Pet." It came out harsher than I would have liked. Harder. "It's time."

"You promised!" she screamed. "You swore I was yours forever! You said it, Donovan, you said it!"

My pained expression met Romeo's, looking at him to do what I couldn't.

Comfort her.

Love her.

Make her feel safe.

In that one moment, I was just a man looking at another man, and we saw eye to eye—keep her protected, get her healed.

I needed to stop being the reason her heart was breaking.

Even though she wouldn't realize it in that instant.

I needed to set her free.

Romeo picked her up off the floor, and she clawed at his body to get away from him, to get to me. Memories rushed through me of the first time she'd reacted the same way she was right now, when she woke up tied to a piano. However, I was hard as fuck for her back then; now, I was just hardened.

A solitary tear slid down my cheek and onto the floor.

Juliet saw it, but I didn't budge.

I closed my eyes and mourned the only way I knew how.

By imagining all those times I asked her to play, and all the times she mended a broken man with her smile.

"Goodbye, Juliet," I affirmed to only her.

"You said you weren't a liar! That you would always tell me the truth! I know you love me, Donovan! I can feel it!"

I didn't say a word.

"Tell me you don't love me! I deserve at least that! If you want to set me free, then scream to me that you don't love me!"

Instead of giving her what she begged for, I spun and left her there.

Breaking.

Bleeding.

Dying for me.

I wondered if she heard my scream minutes later as I collapsed to the ground and tugged at my hair, trying to tear it out of my scalp. I wondered if she realized how many times I stared at the knife in Troy's chest and pondered if it would feel better to just end my story there.

One blade to the heart.

One bullet to the head.

It would be so easy to take my own life, but death was far too good for a villain like me.

An hour later, Elaina walked in, a bottle of Jack in hand. "Thank you."

"For what?" My voice was hoarse from screaming, and it hurt to talk. "Making him finally pay."

She walked over and kicked his body. "The Sinacores are sending a cleanup crew."

"Good for them."

"Where is she?"

I stared into the amber liquid. "Home."

Elaina wisely said nothing as I opened the bottle and tipped it back, waiting for the rest of the men to arrive.

With nothing but my dark, seedy world crumbling down on me.

ould the world hear my heart break? Could Donovan? Why would he? Why? Why take me only to give me back?

I couldn't even feel the physical pain anymore, the trauma, the bruising. Mentally, I couldn't even focus on the shame or fear. All I had was loss.

Loss of him.

Not my master.

Donovan.

My love.

"It's best this way," Romeo declared once we were back at the house, once the doctor had made sure I was okay and treated all of my wounds.

He sent me away.

Master gave me up without fighting for me first. He surrendered like I was nothing more than a toy he no longer wanted to play with.

"Juliet," Romeo barked my name this time. "Did you hear what I said?"

"Does it even matter anymore?" I stared down at my phone. The tears wouldn't stop, and it was like my body was made to create only tears at this point. Until I drowned in a river of them, my head sinking below water with one last thought—him.

Romeo sighed. "He's not normal, Juliet. He did the right thing; he came to us, and—"

"You don't know him the way I do," I snapped. "You don't know what he's been through, how he saved me."

"He fucking kidnapped you!" Romeo yelled, his fists clenched at his sides. "How do you not see that?"

"I see it." I finally looked up. "I know he had other reasons. I'm not stupid, Romeo, but things changed; they shifted. He was … mine."

He shook his head. "Look, maybe you should talk to someone."

I snorted out a laugh. "Oh good, you get back to me after you confess all your sins first; sound good? How many women did you kill after you fucked—"

"Enough," he growled. "Don't make this about me when we both know this is about you. Look … we just got you back, and I don't want to fight for you anymore."

"Then leave," I whispered. "Just go."

"Juliet—"

"Please." I was close to begging. "Please, just go."

Finally, he got up, his breathing loud. "The house is heavily guarded, especially now. All you have to do is text or approach one of the men if you need anything."

"Everyone has their version of prison," I announced more to myself than him. "They all look different, and weirdly enough, it all feels the same."

"What?" He frowned.

"He didn't set me free." I shook my head, then clutched my phone in my hand. "He just handed me over to the jailer—again."

Romeo said nothing.

He left the room.

I started texting Donovan with the phone he'd given me.

> **Me:** I need to talk to you.

Nothing.

It said delivered but not read.

> **Me:** I miss you. Please … please.

Nothing.

Done.

Over.

My villain was gone, never to return again.

CHAPTER TWENTY-FOUR

Six weeks later

I texted him like I always did.

While it said delivered, I knew he wasn't reading them.

I guess it didn't matter anyway. Somehow it had turned into my own personal therapy—texting him, filling him in on the mundane details of my normal life, one I no longer wanted if he wasn't in it.

My stomach clenched yet again.

With a curse, I rushed toward the toilet and puked up my entire breakfast. At first, I thought it was heartache, and then the flu, and now… well, now I thought about all the times we'd had sex.

All the places.

All the instances when we didn't use protection.

He was mine.

I was his.

We wanted nothing between us, condom included.

I knew my mom was concerned every time I rushed away from the dinner table or locked myself up in my room, crying.

The hardest part wasn't keeping food in.

It was keeping the tears from falling.

> **Me:** I haven't been feeling well.
>
> **Me:** Please answer me.
>
> **Me:** I love you.

Delivered.

Delivered.

Delivered.

I threw the phone against the bed and laid back, staring up at the ceiling, not even realizing I was touching the front of my stomach, wishing, praying I had some small part of him.

No one talked about what I'd been through, and they didn't have to ask. They witnessed it every day, from the way I carried myself to the way I talked and poured my eyes out during the day and night.

They knew I missed him with every fiber of my being. I thought a huge part of my family didn't know how to take me. How to understand me, so it was better not knowing. I didn't want to tell them. It was none of their business. I was an adult. A woman. Despite Donovan returning me as if I were nothing more than a child he was babysitting.

I wanted to hate him.

Hit him.

Fight for him.

It was a war I'd lose.

He had turned his back on me when I needed him the most. It was what killed my heart in the end.

I sighed, thinking about all the ways he called me "Pet."

With anger.

With love.

I couldn't hate him if I tried, and trust me, I fucking tried.

My therapist said it was Stockholm Syndrome that I was experiencing. I told her to eat shit and stopped going to her the very next day. I didn't need anyone to tell me what I was going through. They didn't know one damn thing about Donovan and what he'd been through. What he had to endure at the hands of monsters who turned him into his worst nightmare.

"The heart wants what it wants..." Mom whispered as the bed dipped, placing a small box on top of my stomach. "I think you know what to do with this."

Hot tears burned the back of my eyes while I sat up and grabbed the small pregnancy test. "Is it wrong to hope that I am?"

Her eyes crinkled at the sides. "No. I guess you could say I know what it's like to hope for a little girl, to pray every night, and then realize that I won't ever have her. And then one day, your dad confessed something to me, something that you would think would tear a marriage apart."

"He cheated," I answered for her.

She looked away, and her blue eyes focused on the wall. "You know, I think back then I was just so glad he was honest with me right away, and I was able to forgive him, able to look him in the eyes as he owned up to his mistake and say, what do you want? Because at the end of the day, I still loved him, despite how he'd hurt me, but you don't keep someone because you don't want anyone else to have them. You keep them because you love them more than you love yourself. Love is confusing. It's the most precious gift in the world. I wasn't going to lose the man I loved for a meaningless night that he shared with your biological mother."

My throat ached. "So what happened?"

"It was hard." Mom smiled, reaching for my hand. "It was hell, actually, but we fought for each other, and when... when we found out that you were the result of something that could have broken us, we realized that when you forgive, sometimes you're given a gift. You were that gift, Juliet. From the very first day I held you, I knew that you were mine."

My tears seared, sliding down my cheeks. "What was she like?"

"She was beautiful." She placed a piece of hair behind my ears. "She was kind. She was selfless. She loved you very much. It was the hardest thing for her to do. To give you up. Hand you over to us."

I didn't know what to say, staying quiet instead.

"The day we found out she was murdered... It tore your father apart. He wanted to save her. We all did. For you. For Donovan."

"Did you know Donovan before she was killed?"

"He was a sweet boy. Gentle. Nurturing. Life has a way of making choices for you, Juliet. His fate was established the moment he was born."

"Do you think he's a villain? A monster? A sociopath?"

"Sweetheart, I'm married to your father, and with that comes every demon known to man. This life isn't easy, and it's not made for the weak. Your brother is just as ruthless as…" She hesitated for a second.

"As Donovan?"

"We all have a bad and good side. It's what makes us human."

I looked down at the scars on my legs from Troy. They would heal, and eventually, physically, I would be all right; emotionally, I didn't want them to disappear. They were a reminder of what happened when the devil prevailed. They were also a reminder of what I'd felt, seen, lived through.

It all led back to Donovan. He didn't inflict these scars; however, they made me remember that he saved my life, proving to be my hero after all.

"I love you, Mom."

"I know you do, sweetie!" Mom laughed sadly. "And I love you. It's why I can't let you sit here anymore in your room. It's why I told Romeo and your father that this time I was taking charge. They're both silently pouting in the living room, by the way. We'll see how much whiskey we have left after they watch you leave."

My head jerked up. "Are we going on vacation?"

"No." She got up and went toward my closet, and pulled out a bag. "For now, pack a few light things; you'll need new clothes soon. Make sure to take your charger, and don't forget your laptop; though, I'm sure he could afford a new one. That man is richer than two of our families combined." She chuckled. "I'll miss you. Please visit often, call, and don't forget to let us know about the baby. Take the test, and confirm my suspicions." She cupped my cheeks. "You're pregnant … your love made a baby."

"I want the baby so bad, I want—" I broke down into hard sobs. "What if he doesn't want me, though? What if he turns me away?"

"What if he does?" Mom asked. "Then what?"

"Then…" I sobbed. "My life is over."

"No." She clung to my hand and pressed both of our palms against my stomach. "No matter what he says, your life has just begun. The only question is—are you brave enough to fight for it? Your child needs a father, and I have full faith your captor will be your savior. For both of you."

"You don't think I'm weak for loving him and wanting to go back to his life?"

"Weakness is just another form of strength. You were never his hostage, Juliet. If you were, I know with certainty that you wouldn't love and want to go back to him."

"Do you forgive him?"

"I don't need to. You do. This is your life, and you only get one chance to live it how you please. I chose my demons the day I said, 'I do.' Now it's your turn to choose yours."

"Did you forgive Daddy? For me?"

She smiled a huge loving expression. "Of course. Even if we could go back and change things, I wouldn't. His mistake conceived you, and I wouldn't take that back for anything."

I touched my belly.

Thinking about all the possibilities.

Could I do this?

I stood up and walked toward the bathroom. The moment of truth wasn't when I realized I loved him.

No.

It was when I learned that I was pregnant.

Donovan

I was sitting on the bench of my mother's piano, playing Ludovico Einaudi's "I Giorni" for what felt like the hundredth fucking time. For the last seven weeks, this was what I did with my spare moments. I'd sit here and play this tune until my fingers felt as if they were bleeding.

Not for my mother like I did in the past.

No, it was for my pet.

Juliet.

I mourned the loss of her like she had died, and in every way possible, it felt like that to me. She did die. I couldn't see her face except in my memories. I couldn't hear her voice unless I was dreaming. I couldn't feel her skin against my fingers, taste her body along my tongue unless I was imagining her as I fucked my fist to the images of all the above.

It was such a lovely melody, and at one time, it brought me peace. Now it was nothing more than agony. I wanted to feel the pain, the turmoil, the devastation of losing her and losing myself in the process. Because that meant it happened, that meant we existed in one space, in one time, together, and numbing myself wasn't an option.

Every inch of me longed for her in a way I'd never yearned for anyone. She was in my blood, circulating through my veins, trying to breathe life back into whatever was left of me. Her blood was on my hands, her fears, her tears, her love, I owned all that too.

I got lost in the rhythm of the keys, simply fantasizing she was there playing for me, sitting next to me, smiling, putting her hands over mine like I used to do her.

Sometimes it felt as though this was the way I'd live for the rest of my life. In a tower filled with money, power, control, and sex, the seven deadly sins and I were cemented for eternity. Juliet brought so much light to this estate with her smile, her laugh, her innocence. I stole all that from her, and there was no way in hell I was ever giving it back. If I couldn't have her by my side, then I'd have her spirit, her heart; it all belonged to me as well.

She texted.

She called.

She was on my ass, and you'd think it would have granted me happiness, except it didn't. Every day I had to fight the desire to answer her, to claim her, to steal her again. Wrong to dream about killing her brother, so I had no competition.

I smiled.

How fucked up, right?

I didn't learn one damn thing. Every bone in my body wanted what it couldn't have, craving her like a desperate man.

God knows I didn't deserve her.

And the devil wanted me alone with no one.

My thoughts drifted, picturing pet playing for me.

So carefree.

So beautifully breathtaking.

Wishing my day away so I could sleep and dream of only her. Nightfall took over, and still, I played my mother's piano. Spending hours in another world where she and I were together. I shook off the sentiment and took another swig from the whiskey bottle, numbing myself with alcohol before I continued to play. Wondering if she was playing her piano and thinking of me.

The balcony doors were open, and the breeze from the fresh air felt like freezing cold water against my skin. The atmosphere changed in the blink of an eye. The heat of her body radiated onto my back when she suddenly placed her fingers on top of mine like I had with her when she learned I could play too.

We stayed there just like that.

Playing together, the roles reversed.

Now she was my captor, and I was her hostage in every way that mattered.

Play for me, Juliet.

Play.

I squeezed my eyes shut, willing the tears to stay in. Once the song was over, neither one of us moved or said a word, terrified that if we did, this moment would all turn out to be just another dream.

Wishful thinking.

A purgatory for our love.

Thinking my mind was playing tricks on me, or the liquor went straight to my fucking head. I watched as her hand moved, and she placed it over my heart.

It was beating fast.

Without turning, I knew she was smiling. Knowing the effect she always had on me.

Taking her hand off my heart, I brought it up to my mouth to kiss each finger, her pulse, allowing my lips to linger.

She was alive.

Free.

There was so much I wanted to ask, so much I wanted to know. My mind caught up with my heart. There would only be one reason she'd run back to the monster. Her heart was pounding, and as I felt her wrist, my soul felt something entirely different.

I announced, "You're pregnant."

She froze, unable to move from my possessive hold. "How do you know?"

"You're here, aren't you?"

"Was that your plan all along?"

For the first time in six weeks, I smiled against her hand.

Speaking with conviction, "No. This was God finally proving to me that he truly does exist."

CHAPTER TWENTY-FIVE

Donovan

Slowly, I stood and spun to look down at her stomach. Before she could say one more thing, I dropped to my knees in front of her. My mouth was on her stomach, kissing the life we'd created from darkness and uncertainty.

"We can't live without you," she uttered above a whisper.

"And I can't breathe without you."

Gazing up, I narrowed my eyes at her. "This is me, kneeling at your altar, worshipping you, adoring you, and begging you to forgive me for ever hurting you."

"You betrayed me. How could you do that to me?" She was eerily calm despite the tears running down her face.

"I had to let you go."

"Why?"

"Because it was the only way to set you free." From me. From the darkness. From the past. From everything.

"But I'm here now. To fight for you!" she yelled.

I kissed her stomach again. "I know. It was the main reason I gave you back."

Juliet sighed and lowered her head. "I don't understand."

"I needed you to come back to me of your own free will, or else I would have never been able to let go of the fact that I had you taken for me." Stolen her, kidnapped her, made her cry.

She winced, taking in the sincerity of my voice.

I laid all my cards on the table, unable to do anything else but bow before my queen. "Here I am, pet. Showing you my ultimate weakness. It's always been you, Juliet."

"Were you going to tell me the truth about my mother?"

I shook my head.

"Do you want me because I remind you of her?" She looked away, killing my soul in the process.

After I gathered my thoughts, I answered, "I couldn't help but be drawn to you from the first time I watched you play the piano. Your white dress, your hair pulled back, you came to life on that bench with your fingers over the keys."

Tears slid down her face, knowing exactly the moment I was referring to. All I wanted to do was reach forward and lick them all away.

She'd been so innocent.

So pure.

So beautiful.

So mine.

I'd needed her like I needed air. There was no going back after that moment in time.

No regrets.

Only Juliet Sinacore.

"From that day forward, pet. I thought about you, and I knew that I would eventually have you. It didn't matter how fucked up the situation would be; there was no going back for me. I waited and waited and waited for what felt like an eternity. Until finally, you were mine."

"Donovan…" She wept, her lips trembling.

Her eyes showed so many different emotions it was almost hard to keep up.

"You're not my slave, Juliet. You're nothing like the women I've trained. You're strong, resilient. Of all the things you've been through because of me, you've become this life force. I showed you my hell, and here you are burning with me. I've never met anyone like you before. You were made for me, Juliet."

She took a deep breath, wiping away all the tears that stained her cheeks.

"You don't owe me anything. I'm fully aware of that, pet. But you need to know the truth. I owe you that and so much more." It was my turn to take a deep breath. "I fucking love you. Do you understand me? Do you understand how bad that is for a man like me? For the first time in my life, I need someone. You."

She broke down as if overwhelmed by her emotions, by the moment.

I pulled her into my arms, holding her so tight it hurt to breathe.

Longing to feel her, hold her, comfort her.

Fucking love her.

It took everything inside of me not to throw her over my shoulder and drag her onto the bed with me. Again, it needed to be her choice. I couldn't make decisions for her anymore. I took one last look at her.

Silently praying…

She'd let me have my way with her.

Let me, for the first time, love her completely, fully, without reservations, without fear.

Her eyes were shining so bright. Her soft, silky hair was down, blowing in the wind from outside. She was wearing a cream flowing dress that wrapped around each delicious curve, and I wanted to rip it off her.

My cock fucking twitched at the sight of her in my arms like it always did. Because she was mine, my Juliet, my sonnet, my melody, my heart.

The feel of her.

The smell of her.

Overwhelming.

Addicting.

Calming.

She straddled my waist, wrapping her arms around me too.

"I love you, Juliet. I love you so much it terrifies me."

"I know. I love you too. I love you so much it hurts." More tears streamed down her face. "It hurts everywhere."

"You're even more breathtaking than I remember. Show me, Juliet, show me your pain so I can be the one to fix it."

I was relentless, angry, needy. Especially when I wanted something, there was no stopping me. I was insatiable. My hands immediately traveled up her thighs, feeling the scars of what Troy did to her.

"Don't," she murmured, knowing what I was thinking and how I wished he was alive only to kill him again.

She didn't allow another second to pass us by on words I'd never stop repeating to her.

"I love you." I kissed her nose, her lips until I believed she was real and was here against my body, on my cock, in my heart. "You're carrying my child, a life we created. I swear to you that I will protect you both and keep you safe. You're my whole world now."

She always had been.

Always would be.

"What does that mean?"

"I signed the business away," I confessed.

She jerked back, not expecting me to say that. "You what?"

"You heard me."

"When did you do this?"

"The day after I let you go."

"What? Why?"

"Because I can't do it anymore. And most importantly, I didn't want to." Not without her by my side. Now that my revenge was purged from my soul.

"But…" She kissed my lips. "I want you to be my master."

I grinned, licking away her tears. "You'll always be my pet, Juliet. Just because I'm no longer a master for slaves doesn't mean I'm not yours. I'm still the same man who needs both pleasure and pain. I'm still the same villain who wants you to bleed for him. I'm still the same hero who would die for you. Nothing has changed other than my love and devotion to you and our baby girl."

"Baby girl, huh? How do you know it's not a boy?"

"The devil doesn't want two of me. You're an angel, and our daughter will be too. Now, I'm going to tell you how this is going to go. We're going to pick up where we left off. There is no starting over, no new beginnings, no fresh start. The only place we're going right now is to that bed where I'm going to fuck you with my tongue, and you're going to ride my cock, and if you're a good girl, I might let you come."

Her mouth parted, releasing the air she didn't realize she was holding.

"I will never let you go again, pet. Know this now—you came back to me. That's the end. This is your home. I am your master. There are no do-overs. We're together forever, and not even death will part us. I'll find you wherever you are and take you from there too."

She smiled. "You promise."

I grabbed her hand and placed it over my chest. "Cross my heart."

I didn't give her a chance to reply before my mouth crashed onto her, kissing her passionately, adoringly, savoring every last touch, every last tear.

The good and the bad.

It was one giant buildup of weeks of dreaming about her just like this.

At my mercy.

I placed her on top of the piano, deciding I wanted to fuck her first here instead. The last time we were on this, we made a whole new life.

Our baby.

Mine.

Passion and longing radiated off her, sending spasms down my body. Immediately, I knew she was soaking wet between her thighs. I couldn't hold back any longer. I once again dropped to my knees in front of her for a completely different reason.

Growling, I tore off her panties and smelled her warm fucking heat before licking from her opening up to her clit. I sucked it into my mouth, and she ground her pussy against my lips.

My pet loved it rough, and I made her like that.

Only *me.*

It had been so long since I'd felt her in this way, and I could've blown my load from swallowing her taste.

When she came down my face and screamed out my name…

I lost all control.

Exactly the way she craved.

Juliet

I heard him chuckling while he lapped at my bundle of nerves, manipulating them and sucking them in a way that had me panting and breaking to pieces in front of him. He didn't give me any chance to recover. He fucked me with his mouth, tongue, and fingers, over and over again, till I kept coming, my juices running down his face, chin, and neck. Exactly how he wanted me to.

"I want to feel you inside of me."

"Such a needy little pet."

He stood while undoing his belt and then his slacks. Fisting his cock, he grinned in a way that drove me wild and over the edge. I couldn't believe I was here with him.

My family.

My home.

Master now and forever.

I could have cried from the happiness that was washing over me.

The second his lips touched mine, he groaned and opened them. His tongue slid deep inside my mouth, and I moaned, tasting myself all over his lips.

"You taste so fucking good, pet. I will never get enough of your sweet pussy coming in my mouth."

His hands were all over me, roaming, feeling every curve like he couldn't decide where he wanted to touch me the most. I leaned into every touch and sensation, needing to feel him like I needed air to breathe.

I couldn't get enough of him.

Holding onto my hips, he slammed his cock inside of me, jarring my body toward the edge of the piano. Thrusting in and out of me, each thrust more demanding than the last. He fucked me like he wanted to make us one person, one soul, heart.

"Right there… Don't stop… Right there…" I eagerly panted as he gripped onto my hips for leverage, continuing to pound into me. His dick hitting my g-spot from that angle.

"You don't tell me what to do, Juliet. Only been away from me for six weeks, and already you've forgotten who's always in control."

"I haven't forgotten, Master. I'm yours to do as you please."

"Your pussy is so tight, so wet, so fucking good…"

My eyes rolled to the back of my head as my back arched off the piano, coming apart. He stifled my screams of ecstasy with his tongue in my mouth. His hands gripped onto my ass, spinning us around until my back hit the wall so fast that it should have surprised me, but it didn't. It only intensified my desire and need for him.

His dick had me scratching at his back, unable to get enough. He thrust in and out of me, hitting my g-spot with every demanding push and pull.

It wasn't nice.

It wasn't soft.

He was him, fucking me into oblivion.

His lower abdomen glided on my clit, and I threw my head back, matching his hip movement.

I came hard.

His hips jerked forward, and his hand covered my overly enthused mouth, making me whimper. Releasing my mouth, he placed one of his hands around my throat and his other on my hip, gripping hard and applying ample pressure to both. He forcefully and urgently made me bounce on his cock as he pounded into me with no remorse.

I didn't care.

I wanted it all.

"Fuck…" he growled and clutched my hip harder.

My noises grew louder the closer I got to coming apart yet again. He fucked me harder and faster, mercilessly pounding into me, his balls drenched from my wetness.

"That's it, pet … just like that… Squeeze my cock with your tight cunt."

The slapping sound of our skin-on-skin contact echoed in the room.

"Yes … yes … yes…" I breathlessly moaned.

My body shuddered, throwing me off balance from the intensity and overpowering orgasm that only Donovan could ever give me. From the moment he put his hands on me…

I was his.

He didn't stop, and my hands moved to his shoulders as he continued to slam into me. I tried to keep his pace, barely done with one release before another hit.

"Who do you belong to, pet?"

"You, Master. Always and only you."

That was enough to send him over the edge. With a growl from deep within his chest, he blew his seed deep inside of me. If I wasn't already pregnant, this would have definitely done it. I fell forward and clenched onto his neck for support. Panting profusely, I tried to catch my bearings while he placed kisses all over my face, still not removing himself from deep inside me.

"I love you, Juliet. I fucking love you."

"I love you too."

"Later, when I'm done with you. When I haven't stopped until I've kissed every inch of your skin. When I've made you come until you have nothing left. Until you've screamed my name so loud that you can't talk for days. Until I finish you off with only my tongue, fingers, and cock. Then and only then will you know my love."

"Promise?"

His answer was another orgasm brought on by every promise he'd made above. We spent the rest of the night just like this. Where he proved to me just how much…

He was my master.
And I was his.

EPILOGUE

"Your damn brother…" Donovan pouted, arms crossed. "Who the hell does the think he is anyway?"

I just smiled. "Um, a Sinacore underboss, why?"

Donovan still glared. "He's not being careful enough."

"Really?" I sighed. "This from the whips and chains guy?"

He scowled. "She's only two."

"Right, and their little one is only a bit older, and look how well they're playing together." I nudged him and took a sip of my water. The family get-together for Naz's birthday was everything I'd hoped it would be, and it was at our estate.

Our kids, plus our little girl all in the grass sitting, giggling, showing expressions I would have never seen from my brother if he hadn't found his other half.

Which reminded me…

"You want more?" I asked casually.

Donovan froze, slowly turning toward me, his dark eyes narrowing. "Are you asking or telling?"

"Call me pet and see…"

With a growl, he yelled back, "Romeo, kid duty."

Romeo made a face but shot us a thumbs-up as Donovan and I moved through the house toward our master bedroom. Through tragedy, joys were always available; just sometimes, you had to go through the hurt to stop the pain.

Donovan closed the door behind us.

I could feel his heat as he wrapped his arms around me and whispered against my neck, "Something to share, pet?"

I grinned. "I'm pregnant again."

"Just like that?" He smiled against my neck.

"Do I really need to explain the ins and outs of getting pregnant to you, Donovan?"

"Please do. Be as graphic as possible. Pictures preferred, actually. Feel free to act it out; I'll sit."

He moved, but I turned around in his arms, now facing the piano across the room.

Something caught my eye.

Something red.

Red.

"What's that?" Tears filled my eyes as a red rose laid across the top of the piano keys.

"Oh. That." He grabbed my hand and led me toward the piano bench, then pulled it out for me as he reached for the red rose. "It's for you. Because you're no longer just my pet, you're my Juliet, my wife. You're all three, and now I own you with it."

"You do," I agreed, wiping my cheeks.

"Then there's only one thing left for us to do, I guess."

He sat me down at the piano and placed his hands on my shoulders, putting pressure there, keeping me safe, secure. I knew what his next words would be. Grabbing the red rose, he held it in front of my face from behind and whispered in my ear, "Play with me, Juliet."

Not as servant and master.

His partner.

His love.

His soulmate.

"Okay," I said through tears. "I'll play with you, Donovan."

He moved around and sat with me on the piano bench. "A duet, I think would be acceptable?"

"Together." I smiled.

"Together." He grabbed me at the back of my neck and pulled me in for a deep kiss, then released me. "Just no Chopsticks."

I laughed.

And I realized I only laughed like that with him

In his home.

His arms..

With my villain, I'd not only found my laugh but my real home again.

With the monster.

Because in my books? Heroes could go screw themselves.

Give me war.

Give me destruction.

Give me sweet death.

Give me Donovan.

My master for eternity.

The End

WANT MORE?

Did you enjoy Falling For The Villain?
Then don't miss out on our other co-write!

Get to know Romeo Sinacore in Mafia Casanova!

ACKNOWLEDGMENTS

First and foremost, we have to thank God for allowing us to do what WE LOVE, which is waking up every morning and writing, creating worlds, and being able to do it over and over again. Our readers are everything, and we're so thankful that you guys have continued to take this journey with us! To our husbands and Rachel's sons Thor, new little Rorik.

Our assistants Jill, Silla, and Yoda. Thank you for keeping us sane with this one and busting your butts. You worked so hard to make this book what it is, and we could not be more thankful!

Dani and Nina, thank you for loving this concept and running with it, and we are so pumped to have Valentine PR and Wildfire Marketing Solutions to help us with this. Dani, thank you for your hard work! We had to come together, and I think we did it beautifully!

Readers, we hope you enjoy this collaboration. We put our souls into it, and we hope that you walk away feeling like you've just been transported. To Rachel's New Rockin' Readers and Monica's VIPs, thanks for always having our backs and continuing to support, and last but not least, WE DID THE THING!

To all the bloggers & bookstagrammers:
A HUGE THANK YOU for all the love and support!

Last but not least.
YOU.
Our readers.
THANK YOU!!
Without you…
We would be nothing.

ABOUT THE AUTHORS

M. Robinson

Wall Street Journal & USA Today Bestselling Author.
M. Robinson loves her readers more than anything! They have given her the title of the 'Queen of Angst.' She loves to connect with her following through all her social media platforms and also through email! Please keep in touch in her reader group VIP on Facebook, if she's not in there, then she is on Instagram.

She lives in Brandon Fl with the love of her life, her lobster, and husband Bossman. They have two German shepherd mixes, a gordito Wheaten Terrier and a user Tabby cat. She is extremely close to her family, and when she isn't living the cave life writing her epic love stories, she is spending money shopping. Anywhere and everywhere. She loves reading and spending time with her family and friends whenever she can.

Make sure to follow along with her journey on her social media @ authormrobinson or her website www.authormrobinson.com

Rachel Van Dyken

Rachel Van Dyken is the #1 New York Times, Wall Street Journal, and USA Today bestselling author of over 90 books ranging from contemporary romance to paranormal. With over four million copies sold, she's been featured in Forbes, US Weekly, and USA Today. Her books have been translated in more than 15 countries. She was one of the first romance authors to have a Kindle in Motion book through Amazon publishing and continues to strive to be on the cutting edge of the reader experience. She keeps her home in the Pacific Northwest with her husband, adorable sons, naked cat, and two dogs. For more information about her books and upcoming events, visit www.RachelVanDykenAuthor.com